Preface

Love is the foundation whereby the heavens and earth were laid. Love was and still is the message Jesus practiced and preached. Jesus, the night before He was to be taken into custody, falsely condemned for crimes He did not commit, and then crucified for those crimes, reminded His disciples to continue to love one another as He loved them.

Love is the common denominator to and for all human existence. Love is the driving force to live: it is the accelerator that propels people to push and to press forward. Without love, a person is nothing more than a sounding brass or clanging cymbal (I Corinthians 13:1). He or she just merely exists... and that's the amount of it. Though a person may have a heartbeat, a place to call home, or other human associations, if there is nothing to fill the void deep within the soul, life is nothing more than meaningless.

Despite what efforts or energies a person enforces to fill that gaping hole, such efforts prove futile. There is nothing, absolutely nothing, to replace that which God engineered us to be: creatures in need of fellowship and love. This is prevalent from the very beginnings of creation. At that time, Adam had everything this earth had to offer: everything but someone to experience it with. Even God recognized that Adam's heart was not complete.

He needed something more: He needed someone to love and for someone to love him. Out of compassion, God intervened and He created Eve. It was from this single act that the field of genetics was born. It was born out of God's love for man. However, somewhere, somehow, and in some way, the wiring system in man and of man became twisted and thwarted.

Adam was made in the likeness of His Creator, while Eve was created in the likeness of Adam. God gave both Adam and Eve the gift of the disposition to choose between right and wrong; righteous living and sinful living. Adam and Eve opted for the latter. They disobeyed God's commandment not to partake of that forbidden fruit and from henceforth man has witnessed his own depravity

Sadly, unbeknownst to Adam and Eve, the art of deception was developed. Upon disobeying God's commandment Adam and Eve recognized the errors of their ways. Instead of running to God for repentance and restoration, they ran from Him. They hid their shame by first sewing fig leaves to disguise their nakedness and then found shelter beneath the shades of a tree to hide their shame. Since then, man has employed the same techniques and tactics to masquerade his true nature and nakedness. It is the shame of sin.

Though God is forgiving and graceful, the only means by which He can deal with sin is through death. With the advancements in science and medicine, man is just beginning to uncover how genetics are passed on from one generation to the next. It is genetics that serve as a precursor to a person's personality, as well as, physical abilities or lack thereof. Because of Adam and Eve's sin in the Garden of Eden, every person is predisposed to sin. This is the reason the Apostle Paul could write: For all have sinned and come short of the glory of God (Romans 3:23, NKJV).

Sure, there is the age-old argument about whether a person is molded and made through nature or nurture. And both arguments are correct: both are instrumental in a person's overall development. They work in conjunction with one another and are strongly correlated. However, a person would be wrong and remiss to subtract the freedom to choose from the equation.

As you read "Killing Me Softly," we ask that you keep in mind the dynamics of sin and the destructive power sin has over families when they choose to keep it a secret. Though many may believe they are doing the right thing by disguising it, in reality they are doing nothing more than giving sin the occasion to develop into something far more destructive than what a person can personally imagine.

We understand that some scenes may be disturbing to some readers. While we apologize for the intensity of such scenes, we ask that you do bear in mind that much of what you are about read is predicated on fact. The truth be told, some of the stories shared are mild compared to actual events. Our intention is not to appall you, the reader, but rather, to make you aware that such abuses do occur within our society, and sadly, within the body of Christ.

To do nothing, in short, is basically to do something. In other words, people are watering the seeds of sin by doing nothing. Though they may think they are protecting families, they are actually contributing to the slow decay and destruction of the family. As Carl in the novel, I beg you, to report any abuse that you may be personally aware of in the life a person's life.

Who knows, you may very well be the person who not only throws out a life preserver to those being swept away by the currents of sin, but you may very well be the person that breaks the cycle of sin.

Acknowledgments

L. C. Markland

I want to thank Leslie Matheny for accepting my invitation to co-author "Killing Me Softly." She proved her gift in writing, as well as becoming a great friend. "Killing Me Softly" would not be the book it turned out to be had it not been for Leslie's creative mind as well as her challenging me to become a better author.

Leslie Matheny

I was fortunate to have parents that were highly supportive of my academic and creative endeavors. They encouraged me to go back to school in my 40's and obtain a degree in education. My husband Mark, who has also been supportive and patient of my role in this novel, and who said "go for it" when it came to working with Paul Markland.

I also want to acknowledge Gina Rocco and Tonya Keen; both phenomenal mentors in my role as an educator. Dr. Barbara O'Connor, formerly of The University of Akron for her guidance and professional input on writing and Dr. Hal Foster, whose writing class at The University of Akron awakened my passion for creative writing.

I would also like to thank Susan Bishop and Christy Becknell Brown for the opportunity to provide literacy support to students in the Akron Public School. In my role as a reading interventionist I am able to convey my passion for reading and writing to students that need an extra push.

Lastly, I would be remiss if I did not mention Paul Markland. Though we were in high school together, I knew of him, but I did not know him personally. A strange series of events led to our partnership on his novel. I want to thank him for the opportunity to unleash some creative writing skills while walking down memory lane.

A Special Thanks:

This book would not be possible had it not been for the cooperation and concerted effort from fellow classmates from the Akron East High School. Both authors are the product of the Akron Public Schools. Leslie Matheny is a 1981 graduate while L. C. Markland received his diploma in 1983. James Neidert designed the cover of the novel, and Raymond Shook provided the review. Both men were also bred from the class of 1983.

All four contributors went on to pursue higher education as well as contributing to society by becoming professionals in their respective areas of study. A heartfelt thanks goes to each person.

Review

"Killing Me Softly" is a very interesting spin on the classic Romeo-Juliet story. In this modernized version, most of the action takes place in Akron, OH during the 1970s and 1980s from where and when Annie Donaldson and Carl Ericsson meet in the second grade of elementary school to their adulthood. Overall, the story is easy to read but also reminds the reader about the perils and rewards of being in love and how one maintains a significant relationship to their beloved.

There are two protagonists and two antagonists in this book. Annie and Carl are the protagonists while Carl's father, Arthur, and Annie and Carl's relationship are the antagonists and what keeps this story moving and influences both protagonists through the book. I thought it interesting and enjoyed how author's wrote the story from both Annie and Carl's point of view. However, through most of the book, Arthur is a lurking and negative presence.

I was able to relate to this story in many ways. Some to these ideas included, the choices and sometimes mistakes we make in our youth and the trials of being a child in school. For example, being bullied in school and how one handles difficulty. I also felt a connection with how the protagonists and their relationship to their parents changed over time.

The style and the tone of the book mirror the maturity with Annie and Carl. Unfortunately for them, it has a dramatic and darker overtone. In the end, it resolves itself in a very sentimental manner.

This is a love story that I would happily recommend for late teens and adults. It is also a story that considers the emotions of being in love and trying to maintain some degree of control in life as outside influences also bring troubles.

Raymond Shook, Class of 1983

Introduction

For centuries, romance stories have captured the hearts of so many readers. There is something about the passion between people that captivates others. Maybe, in part, that people longed to be loved and to love. Many spend their entire lives in quest of one of the most powerful emotions known to man. Most people get a glimpse of it from time to time, others may be so fortunate to taste it on occasion, but very few couples honestly experience it.

Those who do, their lives are a testament to loves power. Those who have the privilege to see it unfold and to unveil, often refer to the mystery and magic it brings. People tend to open their hearts to the couple. They step outside of the continuum of reality only to take a step forward into the land where fairytales are born. They become an active part in and of the story. They are swept out to unknown seas: waiting, watching, and wanting to see where the direction the story sails.

They experience every possible emotion. Joy, sorrow, anger, guilt, depression, and anxiety become just as real for the reader as it does for those telling the tale. They cheer on the couple as the couple conquers each new challenge. Yet, they cry when the love that had drawn the reader into this romance of romance is on the verge of collapsing.

"Killing Me Softly" is no different. It is a romance for the ages. It is a story of how two elementary students, Carl and Annie, experience what most people can only dream. That is love. Though their love is born in the innocence of their youth, it is tried and tested.

From the moment they set their sights on one another, something special happened. They knew. While Carl and Annie attended the same elementary school, they were from different sides of the track. Whereas Annie grew up in a part of the community known to be safe and secure, Carl, on the other hand, did not have such a luxury. He lived on a street with the reputation of being rough and rugged.

To add to their already fledging romance, Carl had endured the hardships of his father, Arthur. Arthur was as rough and rugged as the street they lived on. He had a reputation for his no-nonsense attitude. His children feared him, while neighbor's regarded him as a man not to be reckoned.

Carl was pitted between two extremes. Does he follow in his father's footsteps, or does he try to change his spots to save and salvage the best thing ever to happen to him? It is Annie. As the story of Carl and Annie moves forward and matures, the reader is caught in Carl's struggle to remain pure and Annie's plight in finding some reason and rationale to keep their romance alive.

To complicate matters, Carl and Annie must endure the harsh realities of sibling rivalry, sports, and even scholastics. What neither Carl nor Annie understood from the moment their eyes first locked onto one another, was that they experienced something most people so desperately seek throughout their life: pure and unadulterated love. Yet, in the end, the innocence of the love that drew them together proves the test of time. Or does it? That's for you, the reader, to decide.

Chapter 1
"Love at First Sight"

The age-old question: What is love anyway? Love is a feeling of affection towards another. It cannot be forced. It may develop over time or it may be at first sight. Love can be a lifesaver or as some may say: *"Love is killing me softly"*.

Carl's Story:

It was the evening of January 2, 1970. The air was warm and a light snow was falling. Christmas vacation had come to an end. Children headed off to bed, as the morning would equate to another semester of school.

Carl was both excited and anxious for school to start. He and his family had moved over break and this would be his first day in a new school. Carl was happy about the move to his new house with six bedrooms and two baths, but he was also anxious about making new friends. Being quiet and rather timid he knew the following morning would be difficult. It would be a restless night of tossing and turning.

That morning in the schoolyard, he stood in a line with several other children outside the doors of Seiberling Elementary School. He stood alone. He stood out like a sore thumb. Seiberling School, one of the largest elementary schools in Akron, Ohio, was a looming brick building. The school was three stories high and sat atop of a hill at the corner of Newton Street and Brittain Road.

Though Carl was among other children, he felt alone. He was the youngest son in the Ericsson clan and was considered by his older siblings as a "mama's boy." And rightfully so: he missed his mom and dad. He longed for the security of his brothers. He scanned the crowd for one of them, but they were nowhere to be seen.

His bottom lip quivered as his soul cried for someone to rescue him from the drama about to unfold. Had he known, he probably would have stayed home. But it was too late. "Ding-a-ling –a-ling."

The bell rang. Carl was swept through the doors and into the halls. He felt like a sheep being led to the slaughter. He headed straight to the office for his room assignment. After morning announcements, Mrs. Schultz, the school principal, gave him a brief tour of the building and escorted him to his homeroom.

Carl was overwhelmed as he tagged along behind Mrs. Schultz. The size of the building was not the only thing that rattled him. He had never seen so many black faces. Fear consumed his tiny little body. He felt like he was being thrown to the wolves. *"Would the black faces he passed in the hallway be friendly? Would going to school with children of a different race make school somehow different?"*

Even though he was with Principal Schultz, he still had a feeling of loneliness. He wanted to flee. He wanted to hide. More than anything else, he wanted to go home. Once again, he could feel the tears welling up in his eyes. Before the tears could spill, Carl and Mrs. Schultz reached their destination. Standing in front of his second grade class, Mrs. Schultz introduced him to his new teacher: Miss. Hillwood.

Miss Hillwood directed Carl to an empty seat. She then asked for a volunteer to be his class partner until he became acclimated to the new school. Right away a hand shot up in the air. "Very well." Miss Hillwood said.

With his head hung low, Carl never noticed that it was the girl he would soon be sitting behind. Her name was Annie.

Carl made his way to his seat in the back of the room. He flipped open the lid of his desk to hide the tears streaming steadily down his cheeks. He hated everything about his new school. Eventually he dried his eyes and looked about the room, that's when he first saw Annie. *"Who was this girl sitting in front of him?"*

The sea of long brown hair caught his eye. He was captivated by Annie's hair. He then noticed her dress. He studied how the colors swirled together to form a distinctive pattern. At first glance, he thought it was a nightgown. *"But who would wear a nightgown to school? Maybe it was a dress she received for Christmas."*

He strained to see over her shoulder, but the only the only thing he could see was the name placard on her desk. It said Annie.

The morning seemed to go on forever. Carl spent most of it daydreaming about the girl in front of him; daydreaming about Annie. His thoughts were interrupted when the lunch bell rang. He got in line behind his classmates and followed them to the cafeteria.

As Carl advanced through the lunch line, he was quickly noticed by one of the cooks. "You're new aren't you?" She asked. Carl just stood in silence. Taking his lunch tray, he followed the line of students into the gymnasium now converted into a cafeteria.

He looked around the cavernous room looking for a friendly face. Carl felt his eyes starting to burn again. Not only that, but he felt like everybody was staring at him. But as quickly as the tears flowed down his cheeks, they dried up.

It was the girl who volunteered to escort him around the school. It was Annie! Annie and another girl were heading toward him. "Come and sit with us Carl," Annie said. "I'm your buddy and have to show you around anyways."

"Annie is my lifesaver!" Carl thought. His eyes lit up. A smile danced upon his heart and within his heart. Carl had already memorized every strand of hair on the back of her head. Now he would etch into his memory, her face. He thought everything about Annie was beautiful.

Carl had an immediate crush. Everything about Annie was perfect. Her smile could illuminate the darkest of souls and her eyes were magnetic. Carl stared into her hazel eyes. Carl had heard about love at first sight. He wasn't quite sure what it meant, but right then at that moment, he was confident that this encounter with Annie was it.

Carl would hold onto this moment for the rest of his life.

Annie's Story:

Annie lay curled in a ball under her covers trying to keep warm. She knew Big Ben was going to start ringing any moment: signaling it was time to get up for school. A cold wind whistled through the bedroom window making her want to stay huddled in a ball. The thought of her feet hitting the cold tiled bedroom floor made her shiver all the more.

The ticking of the clock echoed across her room as the sound of the second hand counted down to the inevitable, Annie turned Big Ben to silence and rolled out of bed. The moment her feet hit the floor, she wished she had worn socks. She scurried to her window to scrape away the frost that had coated it overnight. Annie saw it had snowed while she slept. She groaned: *"Why does it have to snow now?"*

Heading back to school after Christmas vacation had its pros and cons. There had been no snow over the entire break. Annie was bummed that she did not get the chance to use the new sled she got from Santa. *"Of all times for it to snow, it would have to be now. It figures."* She muttered as she pulled off her pajamas and threw on her new nightgown. One of the good things about going back to school after the long break would be seeing her friends and hearing about all the fun things they got for Christmas.

After breakfast the hustle and bustle of coats, hats, scarves, mittens, snow pants, and boots began. As Annie and her younger brother, Paul, bickered over a misplaced mitten, their older brother, Andrew, stood sentry at the door.

Annie and her two brothers made up a small unit in the large army of children that lived on the block. It was the perfect block in the perfect neighborhood Annie thought. Out of the twenty-six houses on her block, ten or eleven houses had kids her own age. There was always someone to play with. There was always someone to come over or someone else's yard to go hang out in. And the Reservoir Park was just within a few steps from Annie's house.

Annie loved going to the park. It was a large park with two swimming pools, tennis courts, fields to run and play tag in, a big playground with swings that looked like horses, and a giant slide! Annie thought how perfect it would be to go to the Reservoir after school. There was a large steep concrete hill by one of the baseball diamonds where she could break in her new sled. In the summer, Annie and her brothers would slide down the concrete hill by using big pieces of cardboard boxes. *"My saucer sled would be perfect for that hill."* She rationalized in her mind.

At the Donaldson house, Annie's brother Andrew stood at the door looking for signs of life on the street. He spotted the three kids from next door stepping out onto their porch and then he saw Pam shuffling up the sidewalk.

When he saw the boy from across the street coming up their driveway, he announced that it was time to go. As the small army marched up the street, the Shelton sisters joined them and by the time they reached the crossing guard, they were twenty members strong.

Marching along in silence, Annie listened to the other kids from the neighborhood talk about the snow and how great it was going to be to break through the new snow that covered the hills and fields. Their mission was to conquer the hill that occupied the front lawn of Goodyear Metro Park.

Since the first successful expedition of Mt. Everest in 1953, the hill at Goodyear would later be termed the "Himalayas of the Heights." Yes, that was their objective. After the final bell announced the day's end of education, they were to conquer the Himalaya's as it called out to them.

In a world all to herself: with it being a school night, she knew she wouldn't be allowed to go to Metro. She would have to settle for the concrete slopes at the Reservoir.

As they reached the schoolyard, the group disbanded. Everyone ran off to line up in front of the entry doors closest to their classrooms. Annie stood in line shivering.

"Why did I wear this stupid nightgown to school?" Annie questioned.

Annie's best friend Jill came and stood in line behind Annie. "Why did you wear your nightgown to school Annie?" She asked.

"It's not a nightgown!" Annie replied.

"Yes, it is, and you're so weird." Jill said jokingly.

Before a conversation could begin, the bell rang, the doors were unlocked, and the kids piled into the building. Seiberling was a looming big brick, three-story school that sat on top of a hill. The school could be seen from miles away because it sat on the highest elevation in Akron, Ohio. Atop of the school sat Newton the Owl: a six foot cooper owl that had weathered over the years. Its greenish-blue coat bore witness to its age. If you did not know the name of this particular school, you knew it as *"the school with the owl".*

As Annie entered the building, the aroma of freshly waxed floors lingered in the air. The papers hanging on the walls danced about the hallways as blasts of cold wind blew in from the open doors.

Students walked gingerly so as not to fall from the slippery puddles. By the time the two girls reached the second floor, they were huffing and puffing. Annie took off her boots and put her coat in the cloakroom. She found her seat and excitedly joined conversations with girlfriends she had not seen over Christmas vacation.

Miss Hillwood, Annie's second-grade teacher was calling roll when the principal showed up at the door. With her was a skinny little boy Annie had never seen before. She could sense he had been crying. She felt sad for him. Miss Hillwood introduced Carl to the class. She asked for a volunteer to show him around the school and to teach him the procedures in the classroom. Right away Annie shot her hand up. *"Oh, he is so cute!"* Annie thought to herself.

Being somewhat quiet herself, Annie knew it would be tough to carry on a conversation with someone she didn't know. During lunch, Annie noticed Carl as he looked for a place to sit. She remembered it was her responsibility to show this skinny kid the ropes so she invited Carl to sit with her and Jill. He couldn't believe it. All morning he sat in Miss. Hillwood's class memorizing every strand of Annie's hair. Now she has requested his presence at the lunch table.

Annie and Jill then pelted Carl with questions about who he was, where his family came from, what he likes to do, his favorite foods and so on. Annie gave Carl the dish on the nice kids versus the mean ones. When the bell for recess rang, the three of them headed to the playground, where Annie and Jill continued their litany of advice for Carl, neighborhood news, and questions about his move over Christmas vacation.

Annie figured her friendship with Carl would be short-lived. She knew he would probably fall in with the boys, but for now, she didn't care. He seemed down to earth. He was friendly. He was cute. And for Annie, that was all that mattered at that very moment.

"Oh, and Carl, here is the most important thing to remember," Annie said as she pointed to a boy on the playground wearing a big brown CPO. "Stay away from him. He is really mean. He is a bully and even beats up third-graders!"

The final bell rang announcing the end of the school day. Students hurried home to finish their homework before they set their sights on the "Himalayas of the Heights:" everyone except Annie. The building was fairly empty by the time Annie got her coat and book bag. She stayed in the classroom to clean the chalkboard erasers for Miss Hillwood.

At the end of every school day the janitor turned on a vacuum system that ran through each classroom. There was a little hole in the wall covered by a metal door that flipped to the side. When the little door opened, anything in front of it was sucked into a series of ductwork that led to nowhere.

Annie ran the erasers in front of the hole until all the chalkboard dust was suctioned off. Chalkboard dust was not the only thing Annie sent into this secret wind tunnel. To Annie, this was a portal to an unknown world. On the days Annie stayed to clean the erasers, she would send scraps of paper through the portal. Scraps of paper with drawings, doodles, poems, or song lyrics entered the air tunnel from Room 205 to who knows where. She imagined her scraps popping out of a portal in another classroom, or making it down to wherever it was all the chalk dust went. Annie sent off a new poem and ran out of the room, through the hall, and down the stairs towards the EXIT sign.

Never did she realize how this portal to an unknown world would come to represent the letters she would later send via the postal system. They would be letters that bore the first name of its recipient, but no known address of any sort.

Annie walked home alone. She thought about Carl. She thought about the nightgown she wore to school. Annie started laughing as she thought about her outfit. One of the things Annie really wanted for Christmas was a maxi dress. All of her friends had beautiful dresses that reached to the floor. Everyone had one except Annie. She didn't get a long dress for Christmas either.

Disappointed in not getting one from Santa, she did the next best thing; she wore her new nightgown and told everyone it was her new maxi dress. Annie laughed so hard that she cried walking home. She wondered what her mother would say if she knew that Annie wore the nightgown she had made Annie for Christmas.

Annie quietly opened the door. The coast was clear. Her mother was in the kitchen and didn't' see she had worn a long nightgown to school; passing it off as a dress she got for Christmas. She flew up the stairs, pulling the nightgown over her head as she headed to her bedroom. She then tossed it in a heap on her floor. After changing, Annie headed to the kitchen and told her mom all about the cute new boy that came to school that day.

That night, Annie dug out her book of Lifesavers from under the Christmas tree and then she retrieved an envelope from her dad's desk. On the envelope she wrote,

Carl,

Don't be sad. I will be your lifesaver. - Annie

And then she placed the roll of Lifesavers in the envelope and licked it shut. Stuffing the envelope in her book bag, she would slip it in Carl's desk the following morning. *"Would Carl think it was corny?"* She wondered, but she really didn't care. She wanted Carl to be happy in his new school.

Carl's Story:

"Did you make any new friends at school today honey?" Mrs. Ericsson asked.

"Yes, mom, I met a real nice girl named Annie. I'm going to ask her to marry me."

Marie laughed at Carl's innocent statement. She thought to herself: *"Only if true love were possible."* She recounted the many times she believed she found it only to be disappointed.

Chapter 2
"Marry Me Annie!"

Despite having cooties, Annie and Carl became best friends their second-grade year. They both had a little crush on one another, but kept it hidden. They often ate lunch together and on most days played together during recess.

One day in early spring, Annie and Carl stayed after school to help Miss. Hillwood with a bulletin board display. The day was gray and overcast. By the time school let out, there was a severe thunderstorm. The thunder sounded like a a freight train rolling across the sky, while lightning lit the skies: occasionally touching the playground just outside.

Mrs. Ericsson, came to Miss Hillwood's classroom to give her son a ride home. Carl asked his mother if she would give Annie a ride home too. There was no way Mrs. Ericsson could refuse her son's request. She looked at Annie only to see the same thing in her, as her son did.

Carl and Annie climbed into the back of Mrs. Ericsson's car. Carl's mom adjusted the rearview mirror glancing at her two passengers. *"Annie you are a lifesaver."* Carl's mother said to herself. Then she looked at Carl and thought: *"Son, you are going to break some hearts."*

When the school year came to a close and summer began, Carl and Annie went their separate ways. Carl got involved with Little League. Every now and then, he would spy Annie on the bleachers. He believed she was there to cheer him on, but in reality, she was there to see her father. He was notorious for being the neighborhood umpire. Many times, Carl suffered the shame at the plate as Annie's father belted out the worse two words a batter could hear: "Strike Three!"

If he did not see her in the stands, their paths crossed at the pool now and then where they would catch up with how their summer was going.

When school resumed that fall, Carl and Annie were in different classrooms. It would be the same for the following year. Even though they seemed to have drifted apart, Carl always held a special place in Annie's heart. And Annie had a special place in Carl's heart. The flame that was ignited in second-grade only intensified as the two grew older.

They were drawn to one another like a bee is drawn to honey. But neither one expressed their deepest attraction and affection for one another. After all, they were both just young elementary school kids. On the last day of fourth-grade, Annie stayed behind to scrub desks. Hearing the squeals of the kids outside the window, she looked out and saw Carl heading across the playground. "By Carl!" She yelled out the window. Carl turned and waved, shouting: "Marry me Annie Donaldson!" Annie smiled.

Annie didn't see Carl that summer before fifth-grade. She spent most of the summer swimming at Reservoir Park. Annie asked around about Carl, but his friends said that they had not seen much of him either. She missed seeing him around the neighborhood and was anxious for school to start.

Chapter 3
"A Year to Remember"

Annie's Story:

"Oh great!" Annie said, while walking into Mr. Warren's fifth-grade class. *"I'm stuck with Mike Camp."* Over the past several years, Annie had been very fortunate to escape the wrath of Mike; the notorious school bully. Annie had known Mike from the time they were little. He was the cousin of Annie's next-door neighbors and he was nothing but bad news. Now he was in her class.

Carl's Story:

Mr. Warren was taking attendance when Carl walked in with a tardy slip. Mr. Warren directed Carl to an empty seat. Of course, like a stealth bomber, Carl tried desperately to make his entrance without much notice. Some say the road to hell is paved with the best intentions. Before he could take his seat, he hit the floor. Mike decided to divert Carl's attention in a different direction. A foot in the aisle sent Carl flying face first to the floor

Annie's Story:

From the corner of her eye Annie could see a devilish grin forming on Mike's face as he plotted with his crew.

The only other kids that had befriended Mike were bullies like him. Annie looked up and saw Carl. He shot Annie a sheepish grin and then THUNK.... He hit the floor. Mike had his foot in the aisle and tripped him. Mike picked on most of the boys in the fifth-grade. He was mean with his words and mean with his actions. In fact, he was so menacing that some classmates would purposefully step in dog poop on their way to school as a measure to keep Mike away from them.

The class got a good laugh at Carl's expense, but the laughter was short-lived and the class soon went about their assignments. By the time the lunch bell rang, the aroma of pizza hung in the air. Annie's stomach growled. Mr. Warren's fifth-grade class made their way to the lunchroom.

Annie took a seat at the lunch table next to her best friend Jill. Waves of laughter made everyone in the cafeteria turn and look. Annie and Jill saw Mike doubled over in laughter: a lunch tray with its contents flew through the air like a bird soars across the sky. Carl's lunch covered the floor with Carl doing a face-plant in the mash potato's that once rested comfortably on top of his tray. He slowly rose and took a standing eight-count. Carl's blood started to boil and a volcano was soon to erupt. Taking his napkin, he wiped off the mash potatoes that now filled his nostrils and looked for a seat.

Annie felt sorry for Carl, but didn't want to become a target for Mike and his bully crew either. Annie knew embarrassment and humiliation well enough not to get involved in someone else's problem, but this was Carl.

Having a soft spot in her heart for him, that made her take notice. Not quite sure what to do, she sat there and opened her lunch carefully contemplating her next move. She waited to see what Carl would do. Annie had warned Carl about Mike, but that was a few years ago.

Looking in her lunch bag, Annie realized she inadvertently grabbed her older brother's lunch by mistake. The bag contained more food than she could possibly eat. She looked over and saw that Carl was sitting alone with his disheveled lunch tray. Getting up from her seat, she went over to his table and invited him to sit with her and Jill. Once again, Annie came to rescue Carl. And once again, Annie would be Carl's lifesaver.

Carl's Story:

Despite a few bumps and bruises sustained from his trips to the floor, Carl was rather cheerful when he came home from school. "How was the first day back to school Carl?"

"Great, Mom!" Did you see any of your old friends?" She asked.

"Yes!" Carl replied rather abruptly. "Where is the phone book?" He yelled out to his mom.

Carl was a on a mission; he missed seeing Annie over the summer and now she was all he could think about.

"Why do you ask," replied Mrs. Ericsson.

"Just because," Carl shot back. His mind was somewhere between delusional and delirious. He could not stop thinking about Annie. He wanted to call her. He had to call her. For what reason, he could not explain. Agitated, Carl hollered again "Where is the phone book?" Puppy love sometimes brings out the unexpected in people.

"It's probably somewhere in a drawer." Carl's mother said.

Instinctively and intuitively, Carl darted from room to room rummaging through drawers and cabinets as if he were digging for gold.

Carl ripped through several drawers like a tornado ripping across the landscape. Papers flew from every possible drawer Carl could find. Finally, he found what his heart was so desperately seeking; the Ohio Bell White Pages. After flipping through the pages, Carl was disappointed to discover Annie's had an unlisted number. While it was very out of character, it was with that realization, that Carl expressed his frustration in a way that would have woken the dead. He said a superlative that was not appropriate for a boy of that age.

"Carl! What did you just say?" Mrs. Ericsson loudly asked. Not realizing the force of his outburst, Carl knew he had just committed an immortal sin.

He rebounded from the shot he just took: "I was practicing a new word I learned in French today!"

"That's what I thought you said." She stated.

Carl's problems, however, were just beginning. His father came home from work and did what he always did upon returning home from a hard day. He set his lunch pail down and headed for the cabinet. He opened his bottle of Canadian Club and worked on building his biceps by curling a few shots of whiskey to his mouth. Taking another shot from his glass, he saw Carl standing there with the phone book.

"How did you rip your pants, boy?" For a split second, time stood still. Carl remained motionless, and silent. Again Carl's dad said: "I asked you boy!" How did you tear your pants?" Carl pled the fifth. "Boy, I am not going to ask you again?"

Knowing that he had to say something, Carl broke down. He admitted that some bully in class tripped him in the classroom and then again in the cafeteria. Disappointed and disgusted with his son's perceived lack of manhood, Carl's father informed him that if he failed to stick up for himself the next time, he would have to face the fiddler. That was, the wrath of his father.

As the sun gave way to night, Carl lay in bed with his head on his pillow. His thoughts drifted between Annie and the classroom bully. *"Someday,"* Carl thought to himself, *"I'll get them both."*

Annie's Story:

After school, Annie joined her two brothers downstairs in front of the television for a snack. Her brother Paul announced there was a big fight in his class today. "Some kid named Allen beat the crap out of Jerry." Allen was Carl's twin brother. Allen was quite the scrapper. Annie knew who Allen was from seeing him at the park. He seemed nice enough, but she witnessed some of the brawls he had been involved in.

Carl came to Annie's mind. She thought Carl was quiet and cute. She felt sorry for him for the way Mike tripped him, not just once, but twice. She wondered if Carl would become Mike's new target. Annie knew that Carl was from a big family and figured that money was tight and maybe they were poor. That was another strike against Carl. Mike would use Carl's home life as another weapon in his armory to torture Carl. And Annie knew it.

Carl and his family lived behind the school at the bottom of the Newton Street hill. It was a neighborhood considered off limits to most kids. It was a part of the Heights where Annie was not allowed to go. Annie thought that Carl was gentle and kind. She was afraid that Mike was going to turn him into something that he was not.

Annie needed to remind Carl about avoiding Mike. Mike would make Carl's year miserable. On several occasions, Annie intervened to be Carl's lifesaver.

"Lifesaver!" Annie thought. Digging in her pocket for a quarter, she headed to Dutt's Drugstore and picked up a roll of Cherry Lifesavers. "To cheer you up" Annie wrote on a piece of paper and wrapped it around the Lifesavers. She would leave the note inside Carl's desk.

"But we're older now" Annie thought. *"Would Carl believe a roll of candy could save him? Carl would think it was totally corny and stupid."* The thought made Annie's face flush. Either way, she was sure that Carl would at least like the candy. She hoped Carl wouldn't show the envelope to anyone else. In the wrong hands, Annie knew her gesture could be turned into something ugly and embarrassing. She stuck the envelope in her book bag and headed off to bed.

Carl's Story:

When Carl woke the next morning, he could not wait to get to school. He lacked the terminology to describe his feelings for Annie. The mere thought of seeing her conquered his fear of another run in with Mike. But unbeknownst to Carl, on this beautiful fall day, things would go from good to bad—and—from bad to worse.

Though shy, Carl was contemplating how and what he might do to capture Annie's attention. He thought that by looking sharp, Annie would be impressed. Riffling through his closet and then his dresser, he had to find the perfect outfit. He had to look like a fox.

Ahhh! There they were: the pants. They were the perfect pants to complete the look. They were buried under a pile of other pants so neatly stacked in a dresser drawer. Carl's mother gave him a pair of these trendy plaid polyester pants. They were the hip male fashion of the time. Pulling the pants out of his dresser, the pursuit of the foxy look was about to turn sour and fly south. It was here that an avalanche was soon to be awakened from the snow-covered canyon of Carl's world. There was no stopping the avalanche soon to come.

The pants were too small. They were too tight and too short. He could barely get them to fasten around his waist. Mrs. Ericsson picked them up over the summer before school started and failed to take into account that he might go through a growth spurt. The plaid pants were the only thing in Carl's arsenal of clothing that he honestly believed would impress a stylish girl like Annie. Well, Carl knew the kids at school would chide him for wearing what was then termed "floods," but he didn't care. All he could think about was how cool he would look in front of Annie.

In his quest to acquire the foxy wardrobe the avalanche moved a foot or so forward when his mother insisted that he complete his look by wearing one of the vests she crocheted for him. The embarrassment of the "floods" coupled with the vest was too much.

Students at school would know that he came from a poor family. *"How many kids honestly wear vests made out of yarn?"* Carl murmured to himself. Sure, it was impressive to the teachers who grew up during the Great Depression. They could appreciate the time and energy it took Carl's mother to knit together such a fine piece of clothing. But this was not the Great Depression. This was the 70's. And like every era, fashion is everything.

Carl did not want to wear the vest, but his mother insisted. The vest dilemma would ultimately lead to one of the greatest natural disasters ever to occur at Seiberling School. Albeit the 70's, a decade of advancements in technology, science, and politics, the eight-track player, vinyl records, civil rights, free-sex, drugs, and what have you, the laws that protected the rights of children had not caught up to the times. Ten-year-olds had no rights.

Despite Carl's best efforts to defy his mother's request, he lost the closing argument in the courtroom. Carl's father intervened. "You are going to wear the vest your mother made you!" His father demanded. "You hear me, boy? Show some appreciation to your mother! And you better not let any bully bully you." Such words added weight to the snowcapped mountains that would in a matter of hours, come crashing down.

Carl knew better than to argue with his father and reluctantly put on his stupid vest. The walk to school was not a long one. It was straight up hill for a third of a mile but in the vest, the walk of embarassment felt like it went on for miles. Like the morning before, the brothers found their places in line. The morning bell welcomed everyone back for another day of learning.

While standing in line with the other students, Carl made a mental note to make it a point to write to his local representative about children's rights. The whole scenario was not fair. How was it that his parents could inflict such cruel and unusual punishment on a child? Did they not know the rules of the jungle? Surely they had to know the law that clearly stated mankind was built upon the theory of the "survival of the fittest." Oh, the public humiliation soon to take place.

Mike started his onslaught of verbal attacks the moment Carl stepped into the classroom. Carl did everything he could to turn a deaf ear to Mike's words. Inside, he wanted punch him, but not in front of Annie.

There would be no tripping foolishness for Carl today. Mike opted for something more sinister. Mike's stunt was to the point; a tack on Carl's seat. He never saw it coming. The instant Carl sat down, the tack accomplished its desired effect. It jabbed through the polyester pants, stabbing Carl in his left butt cheek. Carl immediately jumped from his seat as if someone lit a match under him.

With Mike's teasing, the embarrassment of the vest, now the tack, Carl could no longer withhold the war that waged within. There was no stopping the wall of snow that came barreling down the mountain.

Mike and his classmates laughed at Carl's misfortune. Mr. Warren did not have time to react to the causal chain of events. Carl had been a quiet and somewhat a model student. However, Mr. Warren's fifth-grade class was unaware of three important particulars.

The first and most important was that Carl was the youngest of his clan. Outside of being taunted and teased by his older brothers, they taught him how to scrap. It was not unusual for a fight to break out in Carl's home.

Secondly, most people were not in tune with the philosophy of Carl's father. A philosophy that Carl's father grew up while living in the hills of Tennessee. It was a philosophy that came straight out of the "Ericsson's Code of Conduct."

For as long as Carl and his brothers could remember, it was drilled into them from the time they learned to walk and talk: "You never start a fight; but you never walk away from one either. And if by chance, anyone of them should lose, they had to face their father.

And lastly, Carl's classmates were unaware that, although Carl was skinny and shy, he had an explosive side.

The moment that tack pierced Carl's rear end was the proverbial straw that broke the camel's back. Carl had enough. There was too much at stake for Carl to let this incident slide.

He pondered just for a moment. *"He wondered what the other student's thought of him; what his father would say if he found out, and most importantly, he thought about Annie."* All three thoughts came crashing together to form the primeval instincts to fight. It was at that time the avalanche let go and let loose. There was no stopping the force that came rushing down the mountain.

Carl went after Mike like a cheetah goes after a gazelle. Before Mike knew what hit him, he was down on the floor where he sustained several punches to the head. Mike was beside himself. Never had anyone dared to take down the master. But then again, there is a first time for everything.

The class looked on in shock. Mr. Warren called for assistance from the teacher across the hall. Carl was immediately sent to the principal's office. He took with him his polyester pants, now ripped in the seat exposing his briefs, his lunch pail, his coat, but most importantly, his pride. It would be another day, or two, or three before he was permitted to return to school. And it would be another day, or two, or three before he could see the envelope Annie placed inside his desk.

Annie's Story:

The hardest part of going to school is the prep work involved in getting ready for school. *"What am I going to wear today?"* Annie wondered as she looked at the sea of yarn and polyester hanging in her closet. *"I wish I had a long dress to wear"* Annie sighed as she flipped through the hangers of synthetic apparel. She so longed for a closet full of hip fashions. She wished that one day she could wear miniskirts with stockings like the other girls at school.

She wanted maxi dresses with granny boots, hip-hugger jeans with platform shoes. Instead, she saw in front of her, synthetic pants with elastic waists, polyester shirts, a few crochet vests, and a Girl Scout uniform. Annie's mother, Mrs. Donaldson was handy with a sewing machine. She took classes at the Singer Sewing Store in the local mall and made a lot of Annie's clothes. Like Carl's mother, Mrs. Donaldson was also handy with a crochet hook. Annie had several vests and pullovers that her mother made for her.

Annie felt rebellious on this particular morning. Not necessarily in the mood for polyester or yarn, she decided to wear her Girl Scout uniform.

"You don't have scouts tonight. Why are you wearing your uniform?" Mrs. Donaldson asked as Annie breezed through the kitchen.

"I didn't know what else to wear and this made it easy." Although Annie didn't put the sash over her Girl Scout dress, she did put on the belt with the attached coin purse.

"I want to buy my lunch today" and she tucked a dollar bill into her coin purse.

From his lookout post at the front door, Andrew announced that Pam was making her way up the street and the kids next door were waiting on their porch. It was time to go!

"Hold on!" Annie yelled as she bolted up the stairs to her bedroom closet. She grabbed a green crochet vest that her mother had made for her, slipping it over her uniform as she made her way to the front door. She slipped on her coat and joined the others on the sidewalk.

The school bell was buzzing as this little army made their way to the school grounds. There was no time to socialize with friends before school so they headed into the building and straight to their classrooms. Annie got a few puzzled looks from some of the girls in her scout troop. "Do we have a meeting tonight?" Jill asked as Annie took her seat.

"No. But I wanted to wear the coin belt." Jill shook her head and again reaffirmed that Annie was a weirdo.

"NICE VEST!" Annie heard a voice behind her saying. She turned to acknowledge the compliment and immediately realized the comment was directly aimed at Carl. And it wasn't a compliment. Good old Mike was at it again. The resident fifth-grade bully in his cool tie-dye shirt and bell-bottom jeans was making fun of Carl's vest.

There were many girls at Seiberling who owned a vest of yarn. But Annie, let alone anyone else, had never known a boy to wear a crochet vest. Her own mother had made several for her, but never made one for either of her brothers.

Annie didn't quite know what happened next. Carl did a nice job ignoring the verbal jabs from Mike's mouth, but something, and it was major, set Carl off. Immediately after taking his seat, Carl was right back out of it. Mike was on the floor and the skinny kid was on top of him. Annie couldn't tell what was happening, but desks were shoved about the room, and curse words exchanged between Carl and Mike polluted the minds of those who heard. Mr. Warren did his best to get in between the two boys.

As quickly as it started, it had ended. Both Mike and Carl were escorted out of the classroom and down to the office. Excited children buzzed about the morning's event. Mr. Warren gained some ground in his classroom by instructing his students to settle down and to open their math books. Annie couldn't concentrate on math. Her thoughts drifted to Mike and Carl.

"What a bully." Annie surmised. She was glad that Mike finally got what was coming to him, but Carl had now exposed a side of himself that Annie wasn't sure what to

make of. Carl had a violent side. He changed from a shy kid to a scrapper.

Carl was a scrapper; a fighter. Mike was a bully, but Carl was a fighter. Annie lifted the lid to her desk and stared at the envelope she had addressed to Carl. *"He doesn't need a life saver with a fist like that."* Annie reasoned. She reconsidered leaving the envelope in Carl's desk.

Neither Mike nor Carl returned to class that morning and by lunchtime, the fight was long forgotten. No one knew for sure what had happened with Mike and Carl. It was rumored that they both were to receive an old-fashion paddling from the principal. It was also rumored that they were both suspended.

"Who gets suspended from elementary school?" Annie wondered. She was worried that Carl might get in trouble from his parents. She wondered if he and Mike would make up or if things would escalate. She wondered what had set Carl off in the first place.

Annie's thoughts were interrupted when the wire on her spiral notebook got caught on a piece of yarn from her vest. As she unraveled the yarn from the wire, she pictured Carl standing there with his crochet vest. She thought Carl was kind of a hippy chic in his yarn vest. How bad could he be if he wore a vest that his mom or grandma probably made for him. *"If Carl wore that hand made vest, certainly he must think a lot of his mom"* Annie reasoned. And with that thought, she quickly shoved the envelope with the roll of Life Savers into Carl's desk and scurried out of the classroom.

Chapter 4
"A Fifth-Grade Fight For The Ages"

Carl's Story:

Mr. Roberts, the fifth-grade teacher across the hall, escorted Carl and Mike down the long corridor. Mr. Roberts had both boys by their arms and served as a shield between them. Carl was to his left: Mike was to his right. Walking through the cavernous building, the only sound heard in the hallway were the footsteps resonating off the walls.

Those sounds were intensified as all three made it to the stairwell that led to the inner bowels of the school heading to the principal's office. Carl's nerves rattled like never before. Schultz had a reputation that instilled fear in the student body. Her name complimented and correlated the silent whispers that ran rampant through the student body. Such murmurs spread fear through each student as blood flows through the body.

Carl met Mrs. Schultz briefly when his mother brought him to the school to enroll him before Christmas break, and then again when she escorted him to his new classroom the day he started. Carl already heard about Mrs. Schulz's infamous reputation for being the warden of this prison for education. Everything about her intimidated Carl: her hairstyle, her dress, her demeanor, and most of all her last name.

Carl knew the name Schultz. Schultz was a dimwitted German soldier from a popular television show called "Hogan's Heroes." Schultz was famous for the notorious line "I know nothing, I hear nothing, I see nothing." The Schultz pictured and portrayed on the television was nothing in comparison to Mrs. Schultz. She knew everything, heard everything, and saw everything. Nothing escaped her attention.

This was the seventies. The tides of social evolution were finally catching up with the times. Women gained the right to vote; abortion was now legal, prayer and the Pledge of Allegiance were removed from schools, Darwinism was gaining popularity in the field of science and subsequently the educational system. Desegregation was declared unconstitutional, and the world was at war.

Times were definitely tough. It was not unusual for some type of civil unrest to break out even in one's own back yard. If any woman was prepared to handle the uncertainty during that time, it was Principal Schultz.

Despite the world's problems, Carl was more concerned about his fate as he headed to the office. Mike was still dumbfounded by the events of the morning. It was about time someone placed Mike in his place. He didn't know how to respond to the situation. Soon he and Carl sat across from one another. They sat motionless and mindlessly awaited their sentence.

Carl prayed that Mrs. Schultz's decision would be swift. His imagination kicked into high gear. The only possible punishment that could bring peace to his racing heart was death. Carl knew that if the Schultz didn't sentence him to the gallows, then his life would end in the hands of his parents. It was not the fear of punishment from his parents that brought tears to Carl's eyes: it was the thought of not seeing Annie for a very long time. Never would he experience the first time he would hold her hand or possibly take her on a date. He would never experience their first kiss.

With a bone-chilling creak, the antiquated door to Schulz's office slowly opened. The moans of the old hinges would send chills down the spine of the most hardened criminals. Carl was the first to face his fate. He would be executed first. Rising awkwardly from his seat, Carl stepped into Schultz's office while trying to bridge the gap between his britches.

Principal Schultz had a strange look on her face when Carl entered her office. She could see the Great Divide that separated one cheek from the other. She could not help but chuckle out loud. Much to Carl's surprise, Mrs. Schultz was very cordial. She politely instructed him to take a seat and proceeded to call Carl's mother.

"Oh, boy!" Carl thought.

Carl knew his life would soon be over. His mother, though filled with much compassion and grace, was a hotheaded Sicilian. He knew she would be furious with him. He knew the methods his mother would soon implore upon him. The greatest weapon was her infamous "guilt-trip."

Yes, it was the deadliest weapon ever used throughout the ages. The proper procedure for instilling fear in a child was found in chapter three of the newly released book: "The Revised Standards For Proper Parenting." His mother mastered the art. In fact, Carl would later realize his mother had an instrumental role in writing the current edition.

His thoughts were interrupted when he glanced out the window. He looked over and saw the park across the street. He thought about the summer he played ball with Annie on the bleachers. He looked out toward the pool and laughed. He thought about the cannon balls he drenched her with. A smiled crossed his face when he recalled how close he came to kissing Annie under the sliding board.

But as quickly as the smile came, it faded. His life was over. He would never hang from the monkey bars with Annie. *"Annie!"* Carl was smitten and tears rolled down his face at just the mere thought.

Those tears would soon turn into a torrential downpour. Oh, how he wished things were different. How he wished that both Schultz and his parents would show mercy on his poor soul. Oh, how he just wished...

What Carl did not know was how his tears could soften the most hardened of hearts. Just as the weapon of guilt had been employed throughout the ages, so too had tears. Schultz finished her conversation with Carl's mother.

Was it the embarrassing attire? Was it the tearful face? Schultz's look softened. For a woman known for executing justice swiftly, there was a side of her that most never saw. It was the side of compassion.

She handed Carl a tissue and informed him that his mother would soon be there to pick him up. Like a diplomat representing the United States in foreign affairs, she then instructed Carl to take the rest of the week off. She further advised him, to by all means, get some pants that fit.

Annie's Story:

Out in the hallway, Jill was waiting for Annie. "Oh my gosh! Can you believe that fight!" Jill said excitedly. "I wonder who would have won if Mr. Warren didn't break it up."

Jill continued, "Do you think Carl will dare come back to school? How can they ever be in the same classroom again?"

Annie stopped listening to Jill's rambling after she heard: "How can they ever be in the same classroom again?" Annie wondered the same thing. For selfish reasons, she wanted Carl to be in class with her. On the other hand, she thought he would probably be better off in another fifth-grade classroom. *"This was all Mike's fault!"* The more Annie thought about it, the madder she became.

Before the bell rang announcing the end of the week, Annie said: "Oh shoot! I forgot something. You just go on without me." And with that, Annie turned on the edge of her heel and headed back to their classroom. Seeing that the room was empty, she walked over to the big wooden desk with the name MR. WARREN on it. Opening the desk drawer, she took out a chunky black magic marker.

"Bully; that's what you are Mike Camp. You are a bully!" And with that thought, she wrote in big bold letters across the top of Mike's desk **BULLY!** She put the marker back in Mr. Warren's desk drawer and scurried out of the classroom.

Walking home, Annie wondered when Mike would be back to school. She wanted him to suffer the embarrassment and humiliation he put his victims through. In a fleeting moment, Annie wondered if she too were a bully since she wanted to embarrass and humiliate Mike, but she reasoned with her conscience that he deserved it.

Carl's Story:

Carl's mother, Marie, came stomping into the office. She spoke briefly to Mrs. Schultz before escorting Carl to the car. The short drive home seemed to drag on forever. Marie was notorious for instilling fear into her children. Carl sat nervously as his mother drove in silence: it was a technique she employed quite frequently. The purpose was to bring about the maximum amount of guilt as possible. There was no end to her silence or enduring it. Her silence coupled with the occasional stares (Chapter Four of the Revised Edition) was more than Carl could bear.

Carl loved his mother. The last thing he ever wanted to do was to disappoint her. He was the youngest of the Ericsson clan. His mother had high hopes for him. Yet, Carl was pitted against pleasing mother, while, at the same time, make his father proud. He walked that line separating the two his entire life.

Pulling into the driveway, she broke her silence. "Go to your room until your father gets home." Carl shuttered at the thought. Though his father specifically instructed him the night before not to get bullied, he had to wait his fate. He earned himself a three-day vacation from school where he would ultimately spend three days following the strict procedures and protocols of "The Revised Standard for Proper Parenting."

"What was to become of him? Would his life end at the age of ten? Would his parents impose the harshest of penalties, violating every right given under the Bill of Rights?" Carl didn't know, but he lay in bed and pondered every possible punishment known to man.

His mind drifted to Annie. He cried a little. *"What was it about her that caused him to be so emotional? How could this little brown-haired girl cause so much pain to a fluttering heart? Girls are supposed to have cooties."*

The hands of time moved ever so slowly as Carl lay on his bed in confinement. Though the sun was known to say Goodnight to the day, Carl still knew it would be another hour or two before his father came home. It was inevitable. The time arrived. Carl heard the rumble of his father's car pull into the driveway. He heard the car door open and slam shut, followed by the sound of his father walking through the front door.

"*My life is over!*" Carl thought aloud.

He heard mumblings as his mother shared that Carl was suspended for fighting. Hearing his father's footsteps ascending the stairs, Carl took a deep breath as the footsteps drew closer and closer.

The bedroom door swung open. Carl's heart skipped a beat. Mr. Ericsson popped his head in the doorway and smiled. To Carl's amazement, his father asked one simple question. "Did you win?"

Shock and disbelief overcame Carl. "*No rage? No yelling? He was going to live!*"

"Yes, yes, I believe I did, Dad!"

His father looked proudly at his young protégé and said: "That's my boy! Now I want you to do whatever your mother tells you to do during the next several days. You hear me, boy?"

"Yes, sir!!" Carl responded. His father closed the door and Carl sat stupefied. "*That's it!*" *He muttered out loud.* "*I am not going to die!*"

Carl would not have been so elated had he known what his mother had in store for him. Death seemed to be the more appropriate sentence. During his suspension, Carl's mom kept him busy cleaning the house, washing dishes, and doing laundry. Carl was sharpening his domestic skills. (Chapter Six of the Revised Code). Every now and then, his mother would proudly beam by saying: "Someday you will make a great husband for some lucky girl."

This was rather counter-cultural and unconstitutional. Carl's father believed that men were to work outside the home, while women stayed home to care for the family and keep the house clean.

Monday could not come quick enough. While serving his sentence, Annie was etched in Carl's mind. She was all he could think about. When Sunday evening faded to nightfall, he gave no fuss about going to bed. Falling asleep would not be so easy. Thoughts of Annie danced in his head. Before he knew it, morning broke. He wondered what the day would bring. Did his fight with Mike ruin any chance he had in winning Annie over?

Annie's Story:

Monday morning came way too soon for Annie. The Catholic Guilt Syndrome set in over the weekend. Annie was feeling guilty about defacing Mike's desk. She knew that no one saw her in the act. Jill knew that Annie had gone back to the classroom, but Annie told no one what she had done. Annie's stomach was in knots. If Mike found out it was her, her life as a Seiberling Owl was over. The humiliation of being busted was too much for Annie to think about. The sinking feeling in her stomach was making her nauseous. She had to get to school and act normal.

With her heart pounding and her armpits sweating, Annie scaled the stairs leading to her classroom. She could hear the buzz of her classmates: some were laughing, while others were making accusations.

The finger pointing had started. Walking into the classroom, Mr. Warren was scrubbing the top of Mike's desk. Mike was huddled in the corner with his buddies talking about finding the person responsible for defacing his desk. They were making plans to do some defacing of their own.

"I bet Carl did it." Someone said.

"Yeah!" Said Mike. "Wait till I see that punk."

Realizing that she just made things worse for Carl, Annie panicked.

"He's been gone. He couldn't have done anything." Annie wanted to blurt out. But she couldn't. She didn't even know what they were blaming Carl for. Well, she did, but they didn't know that.

Thank goodness Mr. Warren interjected. "Mike, we will find out who was responsible. It was not Carl. He has been gone for the past several days."

Annie's knees started to show signs of weakness. She was sure that she was going to be busted. She took her seat and wondered what would happen when Carl walked through the door.

Annie glanced over at Mike's desk. She could faintly make out the word BULLY! The marker would not fully erase. Mike was making a ruckus about sitting in his seat. Another student from the back of the room offered to switch desks with him. The children were starting to settle down and get ready for the day. Annie hoped Carl would walk in as she thought the Life Savers still sitting in Carl's desk. On the other hand, she was hoping he would not show up because she knew Mike would blame him.

"Why did I even do that?" Annie thought to herself. Mike took another desk. His previous one was removed, Annie desperately hoped he wouldn't raise a stink. The anticipation was killing her.

Chapter 5
"A Fight Over Muddy Fields"
Carl and Mike: The Rematch

Carl's Story:

The early morning chatter in the classroom went silent as soon as Carl walked through the door. He was not quite sure how to respond to the silence that loomed. He had already set forth an unprecedented reputation. It was a reputation that he did not desire. Yet, he accepted the reputation that was soon becoming a trademark.

Carl stood just inside the doorway awaiting instructions from the teacher. Mr. Warren was very much aware of how explosive the situation could easily become. Wisdom was on his side. He knew how to diffuse contention in the classroom.

He called Carl over to his desk and then summoned Mike to join them. It was a historical moment as two enemies from foreign lands came face to face to sign an armistice. Both Carl and Mike were not exactly sure what Mr. Warren sought to do as he instructed the opposing parties to do the unthinkable.

Most teachers would have separated the opponents, but not Mr. Warren. What he did was uncommon for the times. He made Carl and Mike shake hands. He then instructed them to apologize to one another. "I'm sorry" were words that most students dared never to say in school: particularly in front of their classmates.

Mr. Warren then rearranged desks and reassigned seats. Mr. Warren situated the desks where Mike and Carl were forced to face one another. Carl was no longer sitting behind Annie. Even worse, he was seated at a different desk. Never would he see or know that Annie planted a roll of Life Savers along with her note.

With the word "BULLY" was still visible on the top of Mike's former desk, Mr. Warren did one more thing that stunned Annie. He took the blame for allowing it to happen. He apologized to the class for not completely erasing it before the class entered the room and then declared that the incident was no longer up for discussion.

Annie's Story:

Annie breathed a sigh of relief. She got away with it. But why did she feel guilty? Was it guilt? Annie felt bad that she almost caused Carl more trouble from Mike. She felt sad that Carl was no longer sitting behind her. She was kicking herself for being the reason Carl had to sit across from Mike. But more troubling was they shook hands, and apologized to one another. Annie was sad at the thought: *"Carl was now a friend with Mike. He would be ruined. He would be indoctrinated into Mike's gang; his gang of bullies."*

Throughout the morning Annie stole glances at Carl. She could see him talking and laughing with Mike. She hated Mike more than ever. She looked in her desk and saw the envelope with Carl's name on it. When the class moved desks, Mr. Warren had asked Annie to take Carl's belongings out of his desk and transfer them to his new seat. It was at that time she retrieved the envelope for safe keeping until she could give it to him upon his return to school. She looked at the envelope and felt a wave of foolishness sweep over her. Carl was a fighter. To Annie, one scrapper became friends with another: for any fifth-grader that was bad news.

When the bell for lunch sounded, Annie headed down to the cafeteria line with the rest of her class. She was anxious to see if Carl would line up with her, but he didn't. He fell in line behind Mike. Annie proceeded through the hot lunch line behind Jill.

"Are we eating with Carl today?" She asked.

"I guess not," Annie replied as Carl sat with Mike and his other cronies. Jill and Annie chatted their way through lunch and then hurried back to their classroom. There would be no outdoor recess today as it had been raining all morning. The playground was a muddy mess.

Annie's mind was not on the Checkers game she was playing with Jill. She wanted to talk to Carl. She wanted to come clean about the desk. She wanted to give him the Lifesavers. She wanted to rewind to Carl's first day of school. However, after seeing Carl befriend Mike, Annie excused herself from the game, retrieved the envelope from her desk and ripped it open.

She tore the envelope into little pieces and threw them in the trash. Sitting back down to her game of checkers, she unwrapped the roll of Lifesavers and split them with Jill. Hearing voices in the hallway, Annie turned to the door and saw Carl walk in with Mike.

What started out as a day of peace and reckoning would eventually spiral in a completely different direction. The winds started to stir the still waters. The ocean that once gave promise to a smooth sailing quickly turned its tides on everyone. A tidal wave was soon to crash upon the muddy beaches of Seiberling.

The ramifications of this day would literally be felt for years. As the sequence of events unveiled, lives would be changed. Mr. Warren did an excellent job of restoring order in the classroom that morning, but it was not enough to stop the locomotive that was about to come barreling down the tracks.

The Good Book clearly states not to let your sins be found out. There is just something about hiding from one's mistake; a person's misdeeds often find a way of resurfacing from the depths of the sea in which they were buried. As so it was on that particular day.

Carl's Story:

Just when everyone thought the avalanche that had rushed down on classroom 321 was nothing but a recorded event in Seiberling history, they thought wrong. It was during lunch that a note was covertly slid down the cafeteria table.

It was folded in half and addressed to Mike. Immediately upon reading the note, Mike's jovial demeanor instantly changed. Those sitting around him witnessed veins in his forehead pop. Anger spread across his face. The origin of the note is still unclear to this day, but it yielded information of the most secret nature. Secret indeed! It revealed Annie's dirty little secret.

The bully in Mike resurfaced as he mumbled under his breath: "Annie Donaldson!" To emphasize his anger, Mike took the note containing Annie's dirty little secret; crumpled it up in his hand, tossed it to the floor and then he stomped on it as if he were putting out a fire. "Annie Donaldson! You are mine!"

Annie's secret was out. Someone witnessed Annie going back into the classroom where she did something so despicable, that even she showed remorse. She took the marker from Mr. Warren's desk and scribbled the word **"BULLY,"** on top of Mike's desk.

The person responsible for "dropping the dime" on Annie never came forward: especially when one considered everything that would take place that fall afternoon. Some say it was Connie, who was notorious for fanning flames among other students, but more importantly, because of her crush on Mike.

Mike sat at the lunch table with his buddies Scott, Dave, and Dan. Mike looked them in the eyes. He then declared it was Annie who scribbled the word **"BULLY"** on his desk. "Guys, what are we going to do about this?" He wanted to strike back: the sooner, the better. He wanted to catch her off-guard. He wanted to strike without warning.

Since the weather prevented students from going outdoors to what could have easily been mistaken as a prison ground, the boys decided that the best time to get revenge would be after school.

Carl just sat there stunned. He sat in silence. Mike stared at Carl and demanded an answer: "Are you in?"

Carl was beside himself. There was no way he would allow any harm to come to Annie. "Sure!" He said confidently.

Carl knew he would be in a better position to protect Annie if he pretended to be part of Mike's gang. The five boys put their heads together planning revenge and discussing how Annie would pay for her dirty little prank. They laid out the plans for the assault. It would take place immediately after school in the muddy fields of Reservoir Park.

Carl's mind spun out of control. He could not focus on anything. He had no way of asking for his brother's help. He knew he would face Mike and the gang alone while he defended Annie. What was a few hours away seemed like an eternity.

When the bell finally rang, students rushed to exit the school. A rumor had circulated among the fifth-graders; something big was going down at the park. It was as if someone had announced it over the school's P. A. System. How was it that such news could spread among the classes, yet never making it to the attention of those in authority?

Annie was completely oblivious. She spent the afternoon with her nose in the books. She did everything she could to avoid Carl. Carl felt that Annie was giving him the cold shoulder. If she only knew the sacrifice he was soon to make for her: maybe she would not have acted the way she did. But, as Carl was soon to discover, chivalry was a dying art.

Annie along with Jill crossed Brittain Road before they came to the crossing guard. They decided to cut through the park instead of sticking to the street. Though they did not know it at the time, Mike was hoping they would do exactly that. He, along with his followers lay in wait just behind one of the shelters; watching and waiting for the perfect opportunity to strike. At least a rattlesnake gives off a warning before it strikes. There was no fair warning for poor Annie. Mike struck and he struck hard.

Before Annie knew what hit her, her face became one with the muddy ground. Showing no mercy, Mike confirmed why he had the reputation for being the school bully. Unable to react, Carl stood motionless.

That tidal wave finally reached the shores. It was ignited by the eruption that took place in Carl's young soul for some time. Carl was infuriated as he watched Annie struggle to get to her feet. The eruption came to a climax when Mike pulled Annie to her feet, ripping the sleeve right off of her coat.

Bewildered, Carl took a step forward. He could not help but feel for Annie. Like any peacemaker, he stood between the two opposing forces. For some odd reason, he did something that threw everybody off-guard. He wiped away Annie's tears and then kissed her. It wasn't just a peck either: it was a kiss right on the mouth. Yes, Carl did it! He kissed Annie! For whatever reason, even Carl was not sure. The crowd that had gathered all howled in unison: "Eww! Gross!!"

Carl turned to face Mike; his once former opponent and now friend. The two of them stood toe-to-toe and eye-to-eye. Mike's henchmen surrounded him. Carl hesitated. He knew the odds were stacked against him, but he acted primitively. He struck first. He punched Mike in the face, sending Mike to the ground for a second time in less than a week. Carl then seized his opportunity to finish what was started some days ago.

Students cheered as Mike got his butt whooped. But that would be short-lived. Scott, Dave, and Dan jumped in. They helped Mike salvage what little was left of his tattered reputation as Seiberling's bully.

No one could ever imagine the pounding Carl took that afternoon. Carl accepted his beating like a man. His only cries were to Annie. "Run!" He screamed. "Run, home!"

Instead of heading home, she ran toward Sandy, the crossing guard, for help. Sandy rushed from her post on the corner of Brittain Road and Ottawa Avenue to break up the massacre. By the time she reached the boys, the brawl was over.

The crowd had disbanded and Carl was left alone laying face down in the mud. His nose was badly bleeding and he had several cuts on his face that looked like they might require medical attention. Without hesitation Sandy walked Carl back to the school. Not knowing what to do, Annie tagged along.

For the second time is less than a week, Carl's mother had to retrieve her son. Principal Schultz could not believe the beating Carl received. Once again, Carl was made out to be something that he really was not—a scrapper. Principal Shultz was beginning to wonder what kind of troublemaker's the Ericsson's boys were going to be.

It was not until Annie stood up to vouch for Carl, that Mrs. Schultz saw a different side to him. Annie had a reputation for being a good kid. It was because of her Catholic upbringing that Annie was known for telling the truth. Mrs. Schultz listened attentively as Annie shared the events that had just transpired.

Chapter 6
"Where Do We Go From Here?

Annie's Story:

Throughout the afternoon, Annie wrestled with a guilty conscience over the marker incident. And while Mr. Warren considered it a closed case, Annie decided to remain after school and confess her crime. She told Mr. Warren that she needed to talk to him for a minute after the school's final bell whistled.

During class, Annie tried to look pre-occupied. She kept her nose buried in books, glancing over at Carl every now and then only to quickly turn away whenever he caught her staring at him. Annie tried to convince herself that she didn't care that Carl was now Mike's friend and not her friend. After all, he was a boy; and boys did boy things and girls did girl things. It wasn't like she was going to invite him over after school to play Barbies. But still, Annie was heartbroken over a friendship lost.

As the school day came to an end, Mr. Warren informed Annie that he had to reschedule their appointment. He asked Annie to come in a few minutes early the next morning. Reluctantly Annie agreed.

As the two girls exited the building, Jill said: "Annie, I have to stop by the drug store on my way home. Will you walk over to Dutt's with me?"

Knowing her mother would worry if she didn't get straight home, Annie declined Jill's offer. "I can't, but I'll cut through the park with you."

Though they were breaking school rules, the girls strayed from the sidewalk to cut through the park. They could see that a small crowd had formed and wondered what was going on.

"Probably some poor sap was going to get their butt kicked." Said Annie.

"Gosh, with all these boys here, I would think Mike would be in the middle of this, but he is nowhere to be seen." Jill said.

Scanning the crowd for Carl, a horrible thought crossed Annie's mind. *"What if it was just a ploy? What if Mike was just pretending to be Carl's friend and was secretly going to beat him up instead?"*

Before Annie could think another thought, Jill was pushed from behind and told to beat it; Annie was tackled to the ground. She never saw it coming. She didn't know who was on top of her. The assailant rammed her face in the muddy field. The mud went in Annie's eyes and up her nose. Tears rolled down her cheeks smearing the mud that now plastered her face. Annie was disoriented. Unable to see what was going on, she panicked.

Mud was shoved down the back of Annie's coat. She couldn't breathe with her face smashed to the ground. Her arms and legs flailed in the air. She could hear voices shouting: "MIKE! MIKE! GET OFF OF HER!" When the pressure from pinning her to the ground was released, Annie scrambled to get on her feet.

"Hey, just kidding, Annie." Mike said as he extended a hand to help her to her feet. As he went to grab for her arm, Annie rebuffed his assistance pulling her arm away. "RRRRIP" Mike was left standing there holding the sleeve of Annie's jacket.

Mike's revenge had gone too far. Annie knew the risk when she defaced Mike's desk, but this was beyond her comprehension. It was mortifying to see Mike holding the sleeve to Annie's jacket in his hand. Feeling shame, embarrassment, and remorse for what she had done Annie was at a loss for words.

Mike stood there speechless. Mumbles could be heard throughout the crowd, something about picking on girls. And then she saw him. Annie couldn't believe it. There with Mike and his three goons stood Carl.

"Dear Lord!" Annie thought as Carl approached her. *"Does he think I was trying to get him in trouble?"* Annie wondered.

Annie flinched as Carl raised his hand to her face. Instead of a punch, Annie felt his fingers brush across her cheek, followed by a kiss. A kiss? Carl planted his lips smack dab against hers. There were "ewws" and "gross" yelled from the small group of kids still in the park.

Annie was still waiting for the punch line. Who steps up and kisses the enemy in the middle of a fight. Annie, thinking it was a dare, didn't know what to do. She wondered if her face was a red as Carl's.

Carl then walked over to Mike, who was still holding onto Annie's torn-off jacket sleeve, and stared him down. Then Carl punched Mike smack dab in the face. When Mike hit the ground, Annie took off towards the water tower to flag down the crossing guard.

By the time Annie returned with Sandy, Mike was gone; the crowd was gone, and only Carl remained. Carl laid face first in the mud. Sandy rolled him over. She gasped when she saw how badly beaten his face was. She helped him up and headed back to the school with her arm around Carl. Annie tagged along walking on the other side of Carl holding his hand.

"It's all my fault. It's my entire fault. I'm so sorry. Please don't hate me." Annie wailed as they walked to the school.

Annie knew her mother was going to worry if she didn't get home soon. Upon reaching the office, the secretary called Annie's mother to inform her that Annie was still at school and not to worry.

Hearing the commotion, Mrs. Schultz came out of her office. She took one look at Annie, one look at Carl, only to say: "What in the world?" She escorted them both into her office. Principal Schultz started to lecture Carl about fighting.

The word suspended was brought up. Annie knew this was serious business, but she started to giggle. She knew Carl was injured and she knew his mother was on her way and that she would probably be steaming mad, but Annie was having great difficulty stifling her laughter. The more she tried to act serious, the harder she started laughing. Tears were rolling down her cheeks once again: only this time, it was from laughing.

Principal Schultz gave Annie "the infamous Shultz look." As the principal stepped out to grab bandages for Carl, she shook her finger at Annie and Carl. "I want the full story when I return." Still holding his hand, Annie looked at Carl. "Where do we go from here?" She asked.

Chapter 7
"The Proposal"

Carl's Story:

Annie's question completely caught Carl off-guard. He was not prepared nor was he sure if she was serious. At present, all he knew for sure was that he just got pummeled. The adrenaline from "the fight" as it would later to be coined started to settle. Every inch of Carl's body hurt: he was sore from the top of his head to the tip of his toes.

He looked at Annie in awe. What came out his mouth next even shocked Carl. There, two mud-covered fifth-graders sat side-by-side, one badly beaten and the other still laughing over what she saw.

Carl softly held Annie's hand and proposed to her. He asked her to marry him. They say love makes people do things beyond comprehension. There's some truth to that saying. Annie just stared at Carl as if he just suffered some sort of brain injury.

Before she could process what was going through her mind, Carl's mother stepped into the office. She looked at her son and was shocked by what she saw. She briefly spoke to Mrs. Schultz before she extended her hand to Annie.

Whether it was by "Divine Fate," or Mrs. Ericsson's desire to make great impressions, or maybe a little of both, who knows. But Carl's mother, knowing that Annie was probably as rattled as her rag-tagged son, asked Annie if she appreciated a ride home. Annie accepted.

Carl literally hit the floor. The thought of Carl's mother driving Annie home again was beyond belief. He was not quite sure if he gained her approval or if that was her way of accepting his proposal. Then again, it really did not matter. He was smitten. He was head over heels, but his young heart had yet to define it.

Adding to the mystification swirling around in Carl's head; the song on the car radio was Roberta Flack's rendition of "Killing Me Softly." The song would go on to become a sensation in the world of music. The timing of the song was perfect and it was point-on. Carl's affection for Annie was "Killing Him Softly."

In his mind, he had proven his affection for her by pressing his lips against hers; taking punches to protect the one he cared so much for, and let's not forget the proposal. As the car pulled up to Annie's house, Carl tried very hard to slip her a piece of paper without drawing further attention to the romance dancing in his head. Its contents provided vital information that would later dictate and define the direction of their future: it was Carl's phone number.

With that, Carl and his mom said their goodbyes and rushed off to Children's Hospital. Carl received five stitches above his right eye and some special attention from the nurses.

Annie's Story:

Annie was wound up as she told her mother about the fight at the park, the ripped coat sleeve, Mike and Carl, and the kiss. "Annie, he sounds like a sweet boy, but you are too young for boys" her mother said. "And Annie, it is not proper for girls to call boys!" Annie tacked Carl's phone number to the bulletin board in her bedroom. With only one phone in the house, there was no way to sneak a phone call to a boy.

Standing in front of her mirror, Annie took a good long look at herself. *"I wonder why out of all the girls in our class, he decided to like me."* Staring deeply into her own eyes, Annie whispered: *"What does he see in me?"*

There would be no calling Carl tonight. Annie would see him at school. Shaking a quarter out of her bank, Annie yelled to her mom that she had to run to the store just a few blocks away.

Annie returned home. She ran to her room and grabbed a piece of paper. She scribbled a note for Carl, sticking it in an envelope with a roll of Cherry Lifesavers. Annie lay sprawled out on her bed thinking about Carl. *"He stuck up for me today. None of my other friends helped me. Not even Jill."*

Annie wanted to be Carl's girlfriend, but she knew there was no way her mom and dad would let her have a boyfriend. At school, Annie would tell Carl that she wanted to be his girlfriend, but when she was a little older. And she would marry him when she was a lot older.

Chapter 8
"Boy, I Will Knock You Into Tomorrow"

Carl's Story:

It was already dark when Carl and his mother left the emergency room. It had been a long hard day for everybody. Carl's clothes were still cold and damp from tumbling on the muddy tundra from which he fought, fell, and failed. Carl looked forward to a long hot shower. Inside the Ericsson house that night, a time bomb was about to go off. Carl was about to receive the wrath of Arthur; his dad. Carl was not the only one who had a bad day.

Arthur was a man whose life was riddled with tragedy and turmoil; trials and tribulations. From the time he was a boy to the time he had his sons, Arthur had faced and fought many battles. The wounds from his past conflicts were never properly treated and, thus, they were never completely healed.

As a boy, Arthur had a rough life. Arthur and his siblings grew up in the rural hills of Tennessee. They grew up in an era where technology had yet to catch up on a simpler time. Most people did not have telephones. The automobile had not made its appearance either. It was the lack of such advancements that contributed to the death of Arthur's mother. She died at home in front of him.

Without their mother and being the oldest, Arthur was left to raise his siblings. The Great Depression descended upon the United States. Things for Arthur were to get worse. His father would soon join his mother as he too unexpectedly died. Subsequently, his family was divided. His brother's and sister's were distributed between his aunts and uncles.

Sadder yet, because he was older, Arthur was left out. Though just an adolescent, he was looked upon as an adult. Like the proverbial redheaded stepchild, he was left alone to face the harsh realities of life. Since no relatives took Arthur into their home, he was alone and abandoned.

He eventually found himself literally living life on the tracks. He traveled across the southern states as he hopped from one train car to the next looking for work and his way in life.

It was not until the United States entered into the Second World War that Arthur found a home. He was drafted into the United States Navy where he earned his stripes as a man of great character and courage.

It was with great pride that Arthur served his country. He was aboard the U.S.S. Enterprise during one of the greatest battles in Naval history. An epic battle of epic proportions: the Battle of Midway. It was this war upon the waves that turned the tides in the United States campaign to defeat the Japanese Imperial fleet. The American Spirit was tried and tested. It proved to the world that it was very much alive. The Navy carried out the unimaginable. They defeated an empire that had not lost a war on the water for over a century.

Yet, as in any great conflict, there have been casualties. Regardless of whether a person lives or dies, there are always casualties. It really doesn't matter. No one ever walks away from such trauma without having to endure the scars or the pain associated or accompanied by the loss of life. Arthur was no different.

To add to Arthur's credentials for serving his country, he was also responsible for wiring the atomic bomb. It was a bomb that would ultimately change the world forever. To do what is commanded is admirable: but to suffer the consequences are sometimes beyond comprehension. So it was for Arthur. It was the turning point that gave birth to the horrors that would haunt him for the rest of his life.

No matter how hard he tried to eradicate his past, it always followed him. Despite his best efforts, they were never good enough. Arthur went on to marry and have children. He was a devoted and dedicated father. Just as he exemplified his love to his country, he also epitomized the same type of love through the sacrifices he made to provide for his children.

He worked long hours at a gas station he helped get off the ground. His reward was long, grueling hours and an hourly salary just above minimum wage.

Arthur thought their family was complete until Marie became pregnant with Carl and his twin brother, Allen. Arthur was half a century old when Marie gave birth to first

Allen, and then Carl. Being a father is hard work: it is even harder when a man, old enough to have grandchildren, has his own den of young lions to raise.

That evening, when Mrs. Ericsson and Carl pulled into the driveway, Arthur had been already home. His day was more taxing than usual as the arthritis in hands flared up from the colder temperatures accompanied by occasional rain. The only thing he had to fill his already empty stomach were a few shots of Canadian Club.

Because she was at the hospital with Carl, Marie couldn't prepare dinner and Arthur was fuming. He matched each shot of whiskey with another stick from his pack of Winston's. Carl losing a fight only added to the fumes that seemed to intoxicate the house. Despite the odds stacked against him, there was no excuse for Carl to lose a fight: this fight. The family already struggled to make ends meet. Now Arthur had to worry about a hospital bill.

Carl's night couldn't get any worse; or could it? The old cliché when it rains, it pours is true. The last thing Carl remembers of that night was the song he heard playing on the radio when his mother pulled into the drive. It was Roberta Flack's: "Killing Me Softly."

"Carl, go get cleaned up" his mother said as they walked into the house. Like two mice creeping past a sleeping cat, they entered the threshold of Arthur's kingdom. Carl tiptoed upstairs. Grabbing a towel from the linen closet, he headed for the shower. Comforted by the warm water, he began to scrub the dry blood from his skin.

Downstairs, Marie tried her best to defend Carl. Arthur was not in any mood or in his right mind to hear excuses. He was drained from the hard day and he was drunk. Carl lost his fight with Mike, and that was that. Arthur threatened his boys "to shape up or straighten out, or he would knock them into tomorrow." Though they never fully quite understood the meaning, Carl was about to find out.

Arthur was disappointed in Carl. He forewarned his boys this day would come. And it came. Carl's father stumbled his way to the closet. He grabbed his slapstick; a piece of metal covered with a leather shell and burst through the bathroom door. The purpose of the slapstick was a means for protection. At this time, however, it was not going to protect, but rather inflict pain. Carl was the target.

With no forewarning, Carl was petrified to bear witness to his father's wrath and to bear the brunt of his weapon. There was no time for Carl to react. His only response was to helplessly fall to the ground as the stick struck him across the head. Everything from that point in time was nothing more than a blur.

Chapter 9
"Carl, Where are you?"

Annie's Story:

Annie arrived at school early to confess to Mr. Warren about the marker on Mike's desk. Unaware of all that transpired the night before, Mr. Warren listened in disbelief as Annie told him everything that had happened at the park after school the night before. Mrs. Schultz poked her head in the doorway asking to speak with Mr. Warren privately. The two stepped out into the hallway. Annie strained to hear what they were saying.

When the bell rang signaling that it was time to come in, Annie waited anxiously for Carl to enter and get to his seat. She had planted the note inside his desk and wanted to see his face when he opened and read her letter. She wanted to tell him "Yes!"

It didn't matter that the "yes" had to wait for twelve years, maybe longer if she went to college. But nevertheless, her answer would be *"Yes, I will marry you."*

The tardy bell rang and Carl's seat remained empty. Principal Schultz appeared in the doorway with Mike, who then proceeded to come in and sit down. Lunch came and went but still no sign of Carl. *"I'll look for Allen after school. Maybe he can tell me what's up with Carl."* Annie thought to herself.

Annie was sullen for the rest of the afternoon. She would have to wait until tomorrow to see Carl. Tomorrow came and went and Carl was still absent. Annie was with Carl after the fight. She knew that nothing was broken, except maybe his ego. Not even his ego Annie reasoned. *"He did get in a few good punches too."*

"Mr. Warren, is Carl sick?" Annie asked. But even Mr. Warren didn't know Carl's whereabouts.

Later that night when Annie got home, she looked at the phone number tacked to her bulletin board. Pulling it off the board, Annie bolted downstairs to the dining room and picked up the receiver. With her finger shaking, she dialed Carl's number. Ring-Ring, Ring-Ring, Annie had no idea what she was going to say, but her adrenaline was pumping and she wasn't backing out now.

"Hello." She heard a voice on the other end of the phone say. Silence, Annie was too petrified to speak. Try as she might, nothing came out "Hello!" The voice said again; this time sounding sterner and more agitated. Annie hung up. It would be another night of wondering about Carl. Annie was too chicken to call back.

At school the next morning, Annie sat with her eyes glued to the clock. Carl had two minutes before the tardy bell. But like the day before, and the day before that, Carl did not show up. Annie heard Mike and his friends joking and half bragging that Carl was whooped so good they landed him in the hospital. But surely it was just some good old-fashioned ribbing between the boys: Right?

When the 3:15 bell chimed, Mr. Warren called out, "Annie, can I see you after school please?" Annie sat at her desk while she waited for Mr. Warren to dismiss the class into the hall.

"You've been inquiring about Carl," Mr. Warren said. "I just got word that he has been in the hospital. I don't know the details, but he will be there for a few more days." He continued. Annie was puzzled. She knew that Carl's injuries did not call for a week at Children's Hospital.

Annie walked home alone. Her eyes welled up as she thought about Carl in the hospital. *"It's all my fault. If I had not written on Mike's desk, none of this would have happened."* Annie couldn't be mad at Mike. Mr. Warren had resolved the problem between the two of them. This was all on Annie. Annie wanted to call Carl's mom, but did she blame Annie too? Tears rolled down Annie's cheeks. "I'm sorry. I'm so sorry Carl." Annie wailed as she walked home.

Annie tried to dry her eyes before her brothers could rag on her for crying. "Mom" Annie called out walking in the house. Remembering that her mother had a dental appointment and would not be home after school, Annie threw her book bag down and ran back towards the school.

She knew Carl lived somewhere down the hill behind the school. She couldn't remember the name of his street, but she was going to head in the general direction. Annie cut through the back of the schoolyard and found herself on Honodle Street. *"Is this Carl's street?"* Annie wondered. She walked slowly and meticulously looking at each house as she walked past. She peered into each window hoping to catch a glimpse of someone that looked like Mrs. Ericsson or Mrs. Ericsson's car in the driveway.

When she reached the end of Honodle, Annie went to the next street over and walked back towards the school on Laffer Avenue. She continued her search for the familiar car or a familiar face in one of the houses. Defeated, Annie headed home.

Again, Annie snatched Carl's phone number off her bulletin board. She dialed his number and this time, she would not chicken out. Before the phone had time to ring, she heard a voice speaking into the phone "Hello."

"Hi" Annie responded. With her voice trembling, "Ummm, is Carl there?" She asked.

Before she could get a reply, Annie heard that gruff voice in the background yelling: "Who is it?" The boy with the receiver then asked, "Who is this?"

"Annie." She said. "I'm a friend from school."

"Some girl for Carl" said the voice on the other end. Annie heard the gruff voice in the background state "Hang up!" She then heard a click followed by a dial tone.

"Carl, where are you?" Annie wondered.

A week went by and still there was no Carl. Annie knew Carl's phone number by heart. She rehearsed the conversation she would have with him time and time again. Annie never got the chance to have that conversation. After the second week went by, Annie dialed Carl's number again.

Instead of "Hello," Annie heard: "The number you have dialed, has been disconnected." Annie was heartbroken. Annie was eager for Carl to get back to school.

School was not the same. Annie missed Carl. The classroom seemed empty without him. Even if Carl hated her, she yearned for his presence. She cried, every time Annie looked at Carl's vacant seat. One morning for no reason at all, Annie flipped open the lid to Carl's desk. Tears rolled down her cheeks when she saw that it was empty. Carl's desk had been cleaned out. Annie wondered what became of the letter and the roll of Lifesavers she had left for him. Annie's heart was heavy.

"Where are you?" She sighed.

Chapter 10
"Sins of the Mother"

From the time Carl's brothers left for school in the morning until the time her husband came home from work at night, Mrs. Ericsson would spend the day at Carl's bedside. Riddled with guilt, she faithfully kept a vigil over her son. *"How could I allow this to happen?"* She questioned herself while seeking forgiveness and praying over her rosary. *"How could I have lied to the social workers?"* Mrs. Ericsson would never forgive herself for helping her husband cover up the incident that landed Carl in the hospital.

Doctor's from the E.R. attested that Carl's condition did not warrant or prompt additional medical attention other than a few stitches he received upon his first visit. There were no indications of the blunt force trauma he received from the beating he took in the park. Carl had been coherent and very much cognizant. However, it was deemed that there was insufficient evidence to prove that something else had occurred between his first and second visits to the hospital.

When queried about Carl's brain injuries, Marie lied. Fearful of the potential consequences of Arthur's actions; fearful of Arthur for that matter, she stood by her husband

and held to her guns. She hid the truth regarding the incident that sent Carl back to the hospital.

Carl's Story:

When Carl woke up some days later, his first words were from the song "Killing Me Softly." As he lay there in his bed, he softly raised his hand as if he was reaching to touch someone's cheek and softly whispered the name "Annie."

Holding Carl's hand, "Yes, honey, mommy is here." She replied. But to her dismay, Carl opened his eyes only to say

"Annie is that you?" Marie had mistaken Carl's call out to Annie, as a call out to her; Mommy. While she was elated to be by Carl's side as he came out of the sleep, her heart was somewhat torn knowing that she was not the first person that Carl called out too.

"No, honey." She tenderly responded. "It's mom."

"Where am I?" Carl asked. His head was pounding.

"You are in the hospital, sweetie." She replied.

"The hospital? How did I get here? Where's Annie?" Carl moaned.

Gently caressing her son's head, "You don't remember the fight in the park?" Mrs. Ericsson asked her son.

Carl cried as he struggled to recall everything that happened. The only thing he remembered was kissing Annie in the park and hearing the song "Killing Me Softly."

Marie realized Carl's memory had blocked out the beating in the park, as well as, the one he received by the hands of his father, continued to disguise the truth by saying: "Honey, don't remember? Some kids from school jumped you in the park."

"No, Mom, I don't. Carl said weakly.

Carl's mother reassuringly told him that he would be okay. When the nurse came in to check on his vitals, Marie slipped out of the room. She ran to the women's restroom and sobbed bitterly. She was thankful Carl pulled through his trauma, but the guilt weighed heavily upon her heart. She knew the truth, yet she still allowed her husband to get away with smacking her son in the head with such force that it almost ended his life. Her spirit shouted out loud: "How dare you? How could you?"

What she did not know is how those two questions would eventually resurface again.

Chapter 11
"Welcome to New Jersey"

Annie's Story:

As the school year progressed, Annie remained on the lookout for Carl. She scanned the mall, the local skating rink, the park, and the neighborhood movie theater. She knew that he lived behind the school and she hoped their paths would eventually cross. Annie would spend lazy Saturday afternoons writing letters and addressing the envelopes to "Carl."

She would drop them in the mailbox on the corner hoping they would magically find their way into Carl's hands. Annie maintained this routine for many weeks. The weeks turned into months. A month quickly turned into years. By the time Annie completed sixth grade, her letter writing to Carl had long stopped and he was a distant memory.

During the summer before starting junior high, Annie and Jill were inseparable. The two best friends spent that summer swimming at the neighborhood pool, riding bikes, and hanging out at the local mall.

Annie changed a lot over the summer. She updated her wardrobe. She trimmed down and toned up. Annie went from a frumpy frame to an athletic build. The boys took notice too. Annie was ready to leave the elementary image behind and move on to the cool and hip junior high Annie.

"Wow, thanks Mom!" Annie said as a new desk was delivered to her bedroom. Not wanting to do homework at the dining room table this school year, Annie asked for a desk for her birthday. She had to rearrange some furniture to make room for the desk. She moved out her bookcase and went to clean up the debris on the floor that had fallen behind it.

"Carl!" Annie said as she spied the brittle piece of paper that he had scribbled his phone number on years ago. Annie had not thought about Carl in a very long time. Waves of foolishness flooded over Annie as she thought about the many letters addressed to "Carl" that she had dropped in the mailbox on the corner. She swept the paper up in a dustpan and threw it in her trash can.

What Annie did not know was that...

Carl's Story:

Upon his release from the hospital, Mrs. Ericsson thought it best to send Carl to live with his grandma in New Jersey for a while. Carl would miss Annie. He didn't get the opportunity to tell her goodbye. He didn't want to go, but Carl was in no condition to argue.

Carl tried to make the best of his time in Jersey. He was grateful for the bond he established with his grandma and the opportunity to get to know his maternal side of the family. He was indoctrinated into the culture from whence his grandmother came.

She was a first generation Italian. Her family migrated to the United States when she was an infant. Not only was Carl continually reminded that he was not an Italian, but rather a Sicilian.

"Sicilians were not to be reckoned with!" His aunt continually reminded him. They were notorious for meting out vengeance. It was a lesson drilled into him on a regular basis. Family was everything. Carl missed his family back home, but he longed for Annie most of all.

While Carl settled in with his grandma, things back home was unraveling. Principal Schultz separated Mike from his group of cronies and broke up the gang. Ironically, Mike was put in the same fifth-grade homeroom as Allen; Carl's brother.

Arthur Ericsson had called for a hit on Mike. Arthur summoned his son Allen to "repay evil for evil." If it meant pleasing his father and protecting the integrity of his twin, Allen was up for the challenge. Unbeknownst to Mike, according to the Ericsson Code of Justice, he had it coming. If Mike thought Carl was a scrapper, he was in for a rude awakening.

Soon after Carl's brawl at the park, Allen caught Mike alone on the school playground. Without warning, Mike was struck from behind. Allen knocked him to the ground.

The element of surprise left Mike disoriented. Allen swiftly meted out Ericsson Justice. Words could not describe the beating Mike received that day. The Good Book states "An eye for an eye," so Allen did to Mike what he was led to believe Mike did to Carl. That is, he sent Mike to the hospital where he then received stitches as well as some special attention from the nurses.

For his heroics "to do unto others, as you would have done unto you," Allen collected a ten-dollar reward from his dad and an expulsion from Principal Schultz. The Ericsson – Camp feud had finally come to an end. Allen joined Carl at their grandmother's house in Jersey. While the boys received consequences for their actions, there were no consequences for Arthur. He got away with nearly killing his son.

Having Allen in Jersey helped ease Carl's feeling of being homesick. For every day over the next two years, Carl would wake up in the morning and go to sleep every night with Annie on his mind. He didn't want to forget her long brown hair, the glisten in her eyes, or the smile that could melt the heart of any young man. And how could he not.

Now Goodyear Heights was a small tight-knit community. It was a community where everybody seemed to know everybody. The mailman in particular was rather knowledgeable of the numerous families that lived in the area. The fight in the park was big news amongst the kids, and everyone knew the name Carl. Carl saved Annie that day. When the mailman picked up mail from the collection box on Annie's street, he knew exactly whom these letters were intended for. The mailman held on to the letters simply addressed to "Carl" and would leave them at Carl's house every week or two. Carl's mother made sure that her son received every one of Annie's letters. Annie; the young girl who was "Killing Him Softly."

After the first year of Carl's departure, the frequency of Annie's letters dwindled. A little over a year later, Annie's letters stopped coming altogether. Carl believed that she had moved on. Carl, thinking that all hope was lost, was happy when his mother informed him that she had enrolled both he and Allen back into the Akron schools and they would be returning home for the start of seventh grade.

Chapter 12
"Reunited"

They say time heals all wounds. While there is some truth in that saying, it does not, nor can it, heal the wounds of a broken heart. For the past two years, there was a gaping hole in Carl's heart. There was only one thing that could ever fill the depth and distance which seemed to be just as deep and as wide as the Grand Canyon, it was none other as his first crush: Annie.

Annie's Story:

Annie's disappointment over not finding Carl was short lived. Annie was a teenager now and she was a student in Goodyear Junior High. Annie was looking forward to making new friends from the other elementary schools. She was looking forward to the variety of classes to pick from. There were classes for cooking, sewing, art, wood shop, swim class, and choir. Annie was ecstatic about joining the track and field team.

And then there were boys! The one thing that Annie wanted more than anything was to find the perfect boyfriend. She thought she had it once and then lost it. Annie often prayed for God to open her eyes to the right boy. Annie wanted a boyfriend that would be her friend. Someone she could laugh and joke with: a boyfriend who thought she looked nice even without makeup. Annie was not frilly. She didn't want to have to dress to impress. She wanted a boyfriend who was just like Carl: someone who thought she was beautiful, even when her face was covered in mud. But Carl was gone and she had no idea what ever happened to him.

Standing with Jill, Annie stopped in mid sentence. *"No way!"* She thought.

"What are you looking at?" Jill asked.

"I swear I just saw a guy that could have been Carl." She replied. Annie lost sight of the boy and dismissed the possibility. Eager to find her homeroom, Annie headed towards the building and up the stairs.

And as luck would have it, the first person Carl saw walking up the stairs of the school, was none other than his Annie. He knew that head of hair anywhere. He had to pinch himself. The second hand of the clock paused.

Carl wasn't sure if he was dreaming. He did not know what to do or what to say. *"I'm going to go for it."* He said to himself. He sprinted across the parking lot and hurdled he stairs climbing two at a time. With his heart pounding as if it would burst through his chest, he wrapped his hands around Annie's eyes and blurted out "Will you marry me?"

Annie panicked when she felt someone cover her eyes from behind. But the minute she heard the words "Would you still marry me?" Annie knew.

She knew it was her sign from God. Spinning around and standing face-to-face with Carl, she threw her arms around him, "Yes. My answer is yes. Carl, it was love at first sight the day you walked into my second-grade class."

Well, at least that is what Annie wanted to say. She had rehearsed that line over and over for the last two years. And Carl was now standing right in front of her and she was speechless. She tried to talk, but nothing came out. She just stood there holding Carl in a bear hug.

Before breaking their embrace, Carl stroked Annie's long brown-hair with his fingers., He whispered ever so softly: "I love you, Annie. You know you are killing me softly?" With that, Carl stumbled as Annie yanked him by the arm and pulled him off to the side.

Carl stared at Annie. Words could never describe what he saw. Annie: beautiful, dazzling, gorgeous, or unbelievable? Annie still had her long brown hair, her sparkling hazel eyes, and that smile. Her smile could easily resuscitate the heart of any boy: but there were some things quite distinct and different about Annie. She had developed into a young lady. She had all of her girl pieces and girl parts. Taking her all in, he stood there for a moment to catch his breath. All he could think about was kissing her. His hormones were going into overdrive.

"Where on earth have you been Carl? It's been two years since I've seen you!" Annie inquired in a demanding tone.

"My mother insisted that I had to live with my grandmother in New Jersey. Something about it being what was best for everyone." Carl replied.

Annie's knees went weak and then she became all choked up. She was in shock. She was mad. But she was crazy about Carl and she didn't know how to play the card that was just dealt to her.

"At your grandmother's, why?" She demanded to know. Annie's eyes filled with tears and her voice started to crack. "Why didn't you ever call me? For two years I looked for you, wondering where you were. I worried about you after the fight at the park. I never heard from you after that night." Annie couldn't decide if she believed him about living with his grandmother or not. Her feelings were hurt and she was mad.

"My grandmother lives in New Jersey. I didn't have your phone number. And besides it would have been a long distance call. I am sorry for not reaching out to you. I was not sure why I had to be removed from my house. I really do not know what sent me to the hospital. All I remember was pulling into driveway. All I was thinking about was us. I heard that song on the radio. Do you remember? It was that song "Killing Me Softly" or something like that. I never forgot about you Annie. You were always in my head and my heart. I was afraid I would never see you again. I believe I am in love with you."

"Every time I heard the song on the radio, it made me think of you, Carl. It used to make me cry and still does. Then it made me want to kill you, but it wouldn't have been softly.

I was really mad at you for just up and disappearing. And I mean really mad! Do you want to hear something dumb?" Annie asked Carl.

"What?" He replied.

Annie told Carl how she sent him letters as if she was a child sending a letter to Santa: she addressed the letters simply to "Carl". There was no last name, no address, just "Carl" on the envelope.

"I used to write you all these love letters and drop them in the mailbox. I have no idea what the mailman did with them all, but I used to send you a letter every week. Some mailman probably got a kick out of reading them." Annie told Carl.

"I was crazy about you and I was so excited about being in Mr. Warren's class together. I was going to tell you "Yes" to your question, but you never came back to school. I went looking for your house. I tried calling you. Your number was disconnected. I missed you."

"So I wrote letters and mailed them off to nowhere".

Holding Annie's hand in his, Carl looked at her and said, "Annie, I do not think that was dumb. I received each of your letters and was deeply moved by what you wrote. My heart seemed to stop beating when your letters quit coming. I thought you forgot about me."

Annie was dumbstruck. She wondered how Carl could have received any of her letters when they didn't have an address or a last name on them.

Not believing him, "No, sir!" Annie replied as if Carl was mocking her. "There is no way that you could have gotten those letters. They didn't even have an address on them." Annie retorted.

"But I did. I don't know how, but they made it my house and my mother forwarded them to me in New Jersey. I still have them and will read one from time to time, especially when I am thinking about you." Carl said.

"Well, I feel kind of silly now. I poured my heart out to you in those letters and I never heard from you." Carl squeezed Annie's hand and said: "I promise you this Annie Donaldson, one day I will marry you!"

Annie not sure if Carl was being serious or joking around as he often did with her, "Stop pulling my leg Carl!" She said with a note of seriousness. Then she asked Carl if he was walking home. "Wait for me after school and I'll walk home with you." She said.

Still holding Annie's hand, Carl put his other arm around her and pulled her close. "I am not pulling your leg." He said. "I have never felt this way toward a girl before. You know you are killing me softly. I would be a fool to let you get away from me again. Of course I will wait for you and walk you home after school."

Annie motioned to Carl like she wanted to tell him a secret. As Carl bent down, she leaned into him and whispered into his ear, "Well then, yes. Yes, Carl. My answer is yes."

The bell rang and Annie told Carl she needed to get to homeroom. Looking at her schedule, she realized that she and Carl shared the same homeroom. "Looks like you're stuck with me Carl." Annie said while waving her schedule at him.

With a grin on his face, Carl placed his arm around Annie's shoulder and said: "Oh, you're stuck with me too Annie!."

He removed his outstretched arm from Annie's shoulder only to take her by the hand. There they walked, hand-in-hand down the dimly lit hallways of the school.

Annie looked up to the Heavens and mouthed "Thank you".

Chapter 13
"Young Love"

Carl and Annie walked hand-in-hand down the hall. It was the beginning of a new day, a new dawn, a new school, and a renewed friendship. It was a romance for the ages. One would never expect two twelve-year old kids to have so much love for one another. But then again, that's what fairy tales are made of. Or so it would seem.

Rounding the corner, they spied Mike at his locker. Carl gave him a hard stare and had a fleeting moment of recognition. Unable to make the connection, Carl could not remember the fight at Reservoir Park that took place two years prior. The boys gave a nod of acknowledgment and for now there was peace between them.

Walking into homeroom together, Carl and Annie did the "disco-shuffle" as they tried to walk among the rows of desks. Their hands still knotted together and laughing at their maneuvers, they managed to find their way to two empty seats next to one another.

Carl and Annie were acting like fools, but neither one cared. It was as if they were the only two in the room. That was, until a blunt force came from behind, separating Carl's hand from Annie's.

"Knock it off love birds." Making the high-5 symbol with his raised hand, Allen, Carl's twin brother, looked at Annie and said: "Put 'er there."

There they sat, in homeroom, with their hands joined together. Years later, they both would look upon that time and laugh. They knew that even an earthquake could never separate them. They knew they were meant for each other. They knew they were in love: a love so great that even death could not sever the bonds sealed so long ago. Had they foreknown the future they faced things may have turned out differently. But, at that point time, all they could focus on was the present.

Carl's Story:

The bell rang and students moved on to first period. Carl sat in chemistry, but his head was in the clouds. He kept replaying everything about that morning over and over. Carl loved how Annie had flung her arms around him like a woman welcoming her husband's return from the battlefield. He liked the feeling of her body against his. Carl could still smell the scent of Love's Baby Soft on his tee shirt. He loved that she said: "YES"

New life was poured into Carl that day. The tender heart that had stopped some years ago, started beating again. The pains of the past were no longer. Carl was a new person with a new purpose. That purpose would be to do whatever necessary to be with Annie. Though he was only in seventh grade, Carl set in his mind never to lose her again. He could not imagine his life without her. She was his Lifesaver. His life would never be complete without Annie in it.

Everything seemed right in Carl's world.

Annie's Story:

While Carl sat love struck in chemistry, Annie sat in math. Annie was wise beyond her years. Annie was practical and she was a realist. Annie thought with her mind first and her heart second. Annie was now second guessing herself. It had been a long time since Annie had seen Carl. The more Annie dwelled upon the length of time Carl had been absent from her life and not bothered to contact her, the more angrier she became.

She also reasoned that girls would surround Carl; a lot of pretty girls of all shapes and sizes. Carl had boyish good looks and he had filled out. He was tall and lean with an athletic build. Carl had a flirtatious smile and Annie took note when the girls in the hall were checking him out. Annie knew that the other girls would mean catty competition. Annie avoided drama at all costs.

Annie also considered how she had been looking forward to junior high and meeting boys. Annie was a little boy crazy. She wanted to reinvent herself as well. Annie wanted to be Ann; just Ann. There would be no more Fat Fanny Annie. Annie had grand ambitions to join the track team that fall and she had spent that summer running laps around the Reservoir Park. The chub was gone, and with that so was that horrible name that was bestowed upon her in elementary school.

Annie had questions for Carl. She would not accept Carl's simple answer that he was at his grandma's."

"How could Carl just show up out of the blue and expect me to drop everything for him? Carl is a jerk. But then again, Allen gave me a high-five. He knew my name. He knew who I was. That must mean Carl talked about me while he was away..' So many thoughts raced through Annie's head.

Annie could not decide which side of the fence she wanted to be on. Annie had read books and heard the stories of people marrying their high school sweethearts; but they were seventh-graders. Annie just had to get Carl off of her mind. She wanted the old Carl, the goofball kid from the summers spent at Reservoir Park back.

Annie recalled the many times she had wished for a do-over and here it was right in front of her. When Annie was younger she hoped to one day have a boyfriend that would be just like Carl but the feeling of abandonment was eating at her. Annie developed a tension headache as Annie continued her mental pros and cons list. It was going to be a long day for Annie; and an even longer walk home.

Chapter 14
"All Good Things Must Come To An End"

Annie wouldn't see Carl again until the end of the day. Annie's heart raced when she saw him waiting at her locker. The smile on his face made the hair on her arms stand up. A chill shot down her spine. Annie couldn't help but smile back. At that moment Annie knew. Her mental dilemma was over. She belonged to Carl. Carl took a magic marker from his binder and drew a heart on Annie's locker.

Carl took hold of Annie's hand as they left the building and asked; "So, what's on your mind Annie Donaldson?"

Carl's Story:

The hours could not tick fast enough for Carl. He could not wait for the 3:15 bell to announce an end to another day of education. The only thing Carl learned that day was how much he had missed Annie and to accept the fact that he was head over heels for her. As soon as that blasted bell sounded, Carl was off to the races.

He sped through the hallways, breaking what seemed like tackles from the other students, as he sprinted to his locker. Carl was known for being tidy: however, as he soon discovered, there were far more important things in life than just having a neat locker. He quickly turned the dial to his combination lock, opened the door to his locker, and then haphazardly threw his books on the top shelf. The sound of Carl's locker door slamming shut could be heard across the entire second floor.

The ball again was handed off to Carl. This time, the coast was clear for him to make it to the end zone. The hall was abuzz with other students busy talking, while others were still trying to figure out how to use their locks. Carl made a mad dash over to Annie's locker. In place of a smile, however, Carl was greeted with what most people would define as a smirk. Yes, it was a smirk. Something was bothering his Annie and he could sense it.

Carl reached out his hand to Annie. She reluctantly took it as they proceeded in silence down the never-ending concrete steps that led students away from the institution that reminded most people of a prison. As they somewhat romantically strolled down Martha Avenue, Carl tried to strike a conversation. Pointing over to his left, "Urban legend has it that there is a train engine at the bottom of that pond." Carl said.

But there was no response from Annie. The couple made their way to Goodyear Boulevard and began their long ascent toward the top of the hill. The silence was killing Carl. *"Killing me softly."* He said to himself. Carl was clueless as to what was bothering Annie. On the bridge that crossed over the railroad tracks, Annie followed Carl's lead and stopped. Carl turned towards her and looked deep into her hazel eyes. They say the eyes are the portals of one's soul and Carl knew something was troubling Annie's spirit. "What's wrong, Annie? Please tell me." Carl asked. But much to his dismay, he was met with silence.

What Annie did not know is that while Carl and Allen were in New Jersey, the brothers learned some tricks of the trade so to speak. Allen spent his time learning how to be the Sicilian who practiced revenge, while Carl, on the other hand, was schooled on the romantic side of his Sicilian heritage.

Towering over Annie, Carl tenderly placed his right hand on Annie's cheek, all the while gingerly moving it toward the back her head. As if he were stroking the head of a newborn baby, Carl proceeded to softly run his fingers through Annie's long dark hair.

Without warning, he lifted Annie's chin upward, and with so much tender care Carl moved his face ever so close towards Annie's. She was completely caught off-guard when he uttered the words "I love you, Annie. And, yes, you are killing me softly," followed by a face-plant of the most romantic kind. He pressed his lips upon hers. What only lasted for a few seconds seemed like an eternity.

This classic Romeo and Juliet scene was soon broken up. Like a referee in a boxing match, Allen intervened, separating the two. "Okay, that's enough, you two. Stop kissing before you make me throw-up." Allen yelled as he plowed through them.

Just as Carl so eloquently drew Annie ever so close to his face, so, too, did he let her loose from his hands. She was startled, surprised, and shocked all at the same time. Though her heart was pounding just as hard as Carl's, her response to this Romeo experience was not what Carl expected or anticipated.

Annie finally spoke and it was not what Carl hoped to hear. Still wrestling with her emotions and feelings for him. Annie turned to Carl and with her hands on her hips and an angry look on her face, she lashed out. "Apparently your grandma was not the only one you saw while you were in New Jersey you jerk. I can't believe I carried a torch around for you all this time."

Annie could feel the tears coming on and she certainly did not want to cry in front of Carl. With that, Annie did an about-face and marched up the hill as if she were a soldier offering support to the other troops. She advanced quickly and caught up with Jill and a few of her other girlfriends that were on their way home.

Annie walked somberly next to Jill. She wanted to turn back and fall into Carl arms, but pride was in her way. In her heart of hearts, she believed Carl was heartfelt. *"How could something so perfect this morning abruptly turn so ugly?"* Annie felt like she was a terrible person. Once again, Carl was hurting and it was her fault.

Carl just stood there. He was speechless. Every muscle, every tissue, and every bone in his body ached. But what was broken the most was his heart. The spigots to his tear ducts were turned on and there was neither anything nor anyone to turn them off.

Allen was, by no means, any help. He punched Carl in the chest only to make matters worse. "Dad's right! You are nothing but a 'mommy's boy.' If you want something to cry about I will give you something to cry about."

Allen raised his fists as if he wanted to brawl. Carl turned and faced his twin brother. Without notice or hesitation, but much provocation, Carl punched Allen in the chest so hard that Allen fell backwards. "Are you calling me a wimp?" Carl growled.

Allen, restraining his tears, muttered: "No, not at all! But don't just stand there! Go after her!"

If Allen said or did anything correct in his life, it was instructing Carl to chase the girl of his dreams; and chase he did. Carl sprinted up the hill as fast as he could.

To make up for Annie's head start, and knowing that the shortest distance between two places is a straight line, Carl cut through yards to head Annie off at the pass.

Chapter 15
"Chasing Down a Dream"

Taking his brother's advice, Carl took off after Annie. Seiberling School was in his sights. He could only hope that his maneuvers were enough to beat Annie and her friends to the playground where he, like a bird that nestles in its nest, sat on the swings.

Carl saw a group of girls heading his way. He prayed like he never prayed before: *"Please, please, let Annie be among them?"* He pleaded. As fate would have it, Annie was part of the gang. Carl could hear her voice excuse herself from the group.

The gang of girls split and went in different directions. With thunder rolling in the background, Annie picked up her pace.

Annie Story:

"You have to be kidding me? I can't believe him?" She mumbled when she saw Carl sitting on the swings.

"Annie!" He called out and motioned for her to come and sit down. Annie walked over and sat on a swing next to Carl.

"Carl could tell by the look on her face that she was still fuming. He felt a storm approaching, but it was not from the clouds forming overhead. It was from Annie. But that didn't matter. He was willing to answer any and all of her concerns.

"Okay, Carl, don't look at me. I don't want to start crying while I'm talking to you." Annie said.

"Annie, I can't help but to look at you." He replied.

"I'm serious Carl. I'm a little peeved off right now, well, a lot peeved off right now. I'm upset. I've been stewing all day wondering if I made a mistake this morning. I'm having all these emotions about you being back and I don't know how to handle them.

"Annie, please talk to me." He said. "What is so troubling that you can't talk to me? Tell me what happened today that changed your mind?"

Carl got off the swing and crouched down into a catcher's position. Taking her hands in his he looked up at her. "Annie, you're killing me here. Please. Please just let it out. I can take it." Carl was broken hearted and Annie could hear it in his voice

Biting on her bottom lip to keep from crying, and so desperately trying not to cry, Annie stood up and tried to slide between Carl and the swing. Still holding her by the hands, Carl refused to let go. He pulled Annie into him, wrapping his arms around her and said: "It wasn't your fault…"

Annie cried into Carl's shoulder. "The whole time we were here – at this school, I wanted to be your girlfriend. You never let on that you liked me except for those stupid 'Will you marry me' lines. And then you just disappeared the summer before sixth-grade. I hung out in the park all summer looking for you. I was so happy to see you in Mr. Warren's homeroom and hoped that you would, you know, be my boyfriend.'"

Raindrops started to fall, but Carl's shirt was already soaked. With Annie's face still buried in his shoulder, Carl stood and listened to her. "Seriously, Carl, how can you ask me to marry you when you acted like I was just a boy from the neighborhood. I had the biggest crush on you. My feelings were hurt because you just passed over me and then show up today, two years later and profess that you love me?"

With a lump in his throat Carl replied to her, "Annie, I just want you to know that I never forgot about you. I fell in love with you on my first day of second-grade. That love never stopped: it has done nothing but grown."

Annie dried up her tears and took a step back. "Well, what happened to you Carl? Why did you disappear the night of the fight in the park? I saw you when you left for the hospital. You were not in bad shape. Why were you in the hospital so long? And why did you go to New Jersey? And why didn't you call me? I can't believe you never tried. I got suspended because of you Carl."

Carl raised his eyebrows. "You got suspended because of me?" He said. "What did you do?"

Annie replied, "I called your house and got hung up on. Then I called again and your number was disconnected. I got caught going through the files in Mrs. Schultz's office trying to find a phone number or address for you. I got in trouble from my mom and dad for that one too."

The wind was picking up and the sky grew darker. "Let's get you home before it..."

Before Carl could finish his sentence, the sky opened up and the rains came down hard. Carl and Annie ran as fast as they could and took shelter under the overhang at the back doors of the school.

"I feel like I've been made a fool of." Annie said. "Do you really think I'm stupid enough to believe that you've been living in Jersey, pining away for me, and then coming back to Goodyear Heights telling me you're passionately in love with me?" Annie demanded to know.

"Annie, I had no choice about going to my grandmother's. I came home from the hospital. Things were a little fuzzy. My mom packed my stuff up and sent Allen and me to Jersey. I used to beg my mom to track you down, but all she would do was forward the letters that were left in our mailbox. She also gave me the note you left at the school with the roll of Lifesavers in it."

With a wink, he said to Annie, "Oh yeah, that's what I missed, the rolls of Lifesavers with your mushy little notes." Annie jabbed her elbow into Carl's side.

"Stop it Carl, I'm being serious."

"Well, so am I!" Carl shot back. Looking down at Annie, "I really want to kiss you right now" Carl said. Annie rose up on her tiptoes as if to kiss Carl, but licked the tip of his nose.

"So much for being serious," Carl said, shoving Annie out from the protection of the roof and out into the rain. "You think that's funny?" Carl teased as the cloud of contention lifted. Carl grabbed Annie by the hand and said "Let's get you home!" Carl could not help but think to himself how the downpour came to represent the cleansing and the renewing he had just experienced.

"We're not done with this conversation Carl." Annie yelled as they went running towards Annie's house. Running through Reservoir Park holding Carl's hand... Annie's dream had come true.

Looking out the window, Mrs. Donaldson spied Annie and a friend running down the street. As Carl walked Annie to the door, Mrs. Donaldson held it open, inviting them in. Soaked to the bone, she declared: "Look at the two of you. You must be Carl, please come in!"

Carl was beside himself. *"This was Annie's mother."* He thought. He was not quite sure of what to say or do. "Carl", she insisted: "Please get in here before you get sick." Carl realized where Annie learned her insistent ways. But the best was yet to come.

"Staying for supper, Carl." Carl was not sure if Mrs. Donaldson was asking or demanding that he stay. Before he could answer, Mrs. Donaldson settled the issue by exclaiming: "Of course, you can. I made meatloaf with mashed potatoes. Let me get you two some towels to dry off."

With water dripping off their clothes, Annie's mom went and retrieved some towels. Annie patted herself dry and darted upstairs to change. Carl just stood there in the foyer.

"Carl, please make yourself at home. Supper will be ready in a few minutes. Annie's dad should be home from work soon. Have a seat on the couch." Mrs. Donaldson suggested.

Somewhere between "Annie's dad should be coming home from work and have a seat on the couch," Carl lost his hearing. He went deaf: yes, deaf. *"Annie's dad, oh no."* He thought to himself. It was too late for Carl to respond. Mr. Donaldson had already stepped in from behind the back door before Carl had a chance to speak or move.

Mrs. Donaldson quickly introduced Carl to her husband. The first words out Mr. Donaldson's mouth were "Carl? Ahhh! You must be the young man that Annie was suspended over."

Annie's father smiled. "The last time I remember seeing you, you were standing at the plate. Did you ever learn how to swing that bat?"

Feeling as though he were put on the spot, Carl sputtered the words: "I suppose so, sir."

Mr. Donaldson was dubbed, "The Mayor of Goodyear Heights". He knew exactly who Carl was. Mr. Donaldson was well known because of his involvement with the youth sports program and high school athletics. Annie and her brothers had to be on their best behavior when out and about their neighborhood.

Mr. Donaldson not only knew all the kids in the neighborhood, but he also knew their parents. It seemed like there were always phone calls coming into the Donaldson house "Do you know what I saw a kid doing?" Nothing got by him.

Mr. Donaldson pulled out his yoga mat, looked at Carl and asked "You still playing baseball for Al?" Sitting in the Donaldson living room, Carl wasn't paying attention to the conversation at hand. Annie coming down the steps sidetracked him.

Carl's Story:

Carl's heart literally stopped as he watched Annie descend the stairs. What she was wearing was not important in as much as how beautiful she looked. Her hair. *"My gosh!"* Carl thought. Annie had pulled her hair back in a French braid accentuating the true beauty of her face. Her hazel eyes radiating a brilliance of an early morning sunrise and her smile had the power to warm the heart of any man. All Carl could do was sit and stare.

Without ever turning his head, Carl made a statement that sent shockwaves throughout the Donaldson home. Mustering up what courage he could, Carl clearly stated: "Mr. Donaldson, with all due respect, sir, I am going to marry your Annie someday!"

Annie stopped dead in her tracks, waiting for the explosion from her dad. Mr. Donaldson interrupted Carl's train of thought by responding: "Well, son, I may now call you son, you have some competition with Robert."

Confused, Carl replied: "Come again, sir, the competition from who?" Carl's full attention was geared toward his Annie.

Annie interrupted, "Oh, he tells everyone "Robert called." And then when you ask Robert who, he says: "Robert Redford. Don't ask."

Annie's brother Paul came into the room. Puffing out his chest and flexing a muscle, he looked at Carl and said: "You jack with my sister and I'll jack with you." Then he faked Carl out like he was going to punch him and said "Man, dude, just kidding. What's up?" Just about then, Mrs. Donaldson announced that supper was ready.

Mr. Donaldson then pointed the way to the dining room only to ask Carl: "Son, I may call you son, are you not going to join us?"

Still mesmerized by Annie's beauty, Carl answered: "Sir, yes, sir."

It was Carl's first meal with Annie's family and he hoped that it would not be his last. They sat there as a family only to enjoy one another's company and the differing stories each child had to share. Time elapsed without warning. Carl looked at the kitchen clock and excused himself. "I must be getting home."

Mrs. Donaldson asked Carl if he would like a ride home. "Much obliged, ma'am, but I think I could make it home before it gets dark." Carl respectfully replied.

"Are you sure, son, I may call you son?" Mr. Donaldson interrupted.

"Yes, yes, thank you very much. I appreciated the dinner." Carl said.

Having said his goodbyes, Annie showed Carl to the front door. He looked upon her as if he and she were the only two in the world. Everything in his heart told him to kiss her, though everything in his head reminded him that was probably not a good idea.

Annie looked at him only to say: "Will I see you in school tomorrow?"

Carl did not even pause to answer Annie's question: "You bet, Annie! I will be there, well before the bell even thinks about ringing. I will be on the steps waiting for you."

He started to sprint home. The rain had dissipated. Carl's thoughts were all to himself. He was on cloud nine and riding high. He just had dinner with Annie's family and even declared to her father that he would have Annie's hand in marriage. All was right with the world. That was, until he hit the corner of Big Bad Bertha's house.

It was there Carl had a chance encounter with a large Afro-American girl known as Big Bad Bertha. Standing in the middle of the road, Big Bad Bertha was the barricade which stopped Carl in his tracks.

Carl was not sure of her intentions, but he respectfully put on his brakes. He looked at her as she smiled back at him. From out of the blue skies that were now forming from a day soon to end, Big Bad Bertha asked Carl: "Boy, are you not afraid to be running through theses streets at dusk?"

Carl, still reminiscing over his romantic evening at the Donaldson's replied: "Nope. Not at all."

Bearing the gold tooth that placated her face, Big Bad Bertha just smiled and said: "You will be, boy! Believe me, you will be." Carl faintly listened to Big Bertha's warnings. He knew he had a far greater battle before him than the streets: he had to face his father.

The interrogation Annie spewed on him would be nothing compared to the one awaiting him when he finally made it home.

Chapter 16
"In Love with Carl"

Robert Redford, Annie couldn't believe that her dad pulled the old Robert Redford on Carl. After Carl left, Annie headed to her room to begin her homework. Switching on the radio she heard the DJ announce "Coming up next, Neil Sedaka, Laughter in the Rain." Stopping what she was doing, Annie turned up the radio and absorbed the lyrics: "Walking hand-in-hand with the one I love. Oh, how I love the rainy days and the happy way I feel inside" Those words resonated in Annie's head. *"That is exactly how I felt tonight."* Annie thought.

Annie replayed the events of the day over and over in her head. She loved how everything had worked out. Annie's parents had met Carl. That awkward first time over went well despite the juvenile behavior of her brother Paul. The day at school was perfect. Annie felt shameful for the way she treated Carl on the walk home. She was thankful for Carl's persistence and patience. Annie's thoughts drifted back to a conversation in particular.

"Are you sure that you really want to be with me Carl? I know girls are going to be all over you this year." After

all, Carl was sweet and kind. He was a fox. How could girls not be all over him?

Annie loved Carl's reply, "Well, let them come. I will just politely say that I am Annie Donaldson's boyfriend. Those words will flow out of my mouth like water flows downstream, my dear." Annie liked it when he called her "my dear.".

"How can Carl be so sure of what he wants?" Annie wondered. *"His parents must have a beautiful marriage."* Annie was curious about Carl's life at home and couldn't wait to meet his family. She had met Allen of course and she met Carl's mother the two times she drove Annie home. But Carl was one of five boys. Carl's mom must be a saint Annie thought.

Annie loved her home life. Her dad yelled a bit, but mostly when Annie or her brothers were misbehaving or when they received bad grades on their report cards. The Donaldson's went to church every Saturday night, followed by dinner out on the town.

Annie's father supported his children in sports, dance, karate lessons, school activities: you name it, he supported it. There were annual picnics and Christmas parties with the Goodyear employees. The Donaldson family completed annual hiking sprees together. Every Tuesday night Annie's dad loaded up the family station wagon and headed to the big library in downtown Akron. On Friday nights he took his sons and their friends swimming at the YMCA.

Annie's mother worked for the local school system. She was active in the PTA. She carted her children all over town making sure they got to the places that they needed to be; track meets, football games, bowling league, karate lessons, and so on.

Now Carl would be a part of the family's activities. I will definitely invite him over for dinner again. HAUNTED HOUSES! Yes, haunted houses. Annie hoped that Carl wouldn't be a sissy and that he would hit the haunted house circuit when her dad took them every fall.

"I can pretend to be scared and Carl will be my hero". Annie giggled thinking that she would stock up on a few rolls of Lifesavers, telling Carl that he saved her from the haunted houses

Annie's thoughts were interrupted when her brother opened her bedroom door, "Man Annie, I didn't know you liked Carl." He said. "Be careful, his brother is a punk. And he likes to beat people up."

"Yeah, I know." Annie replied. "But he's nice to me, so that's all that matters." She said.

Shooing her brother out of her room, Annie pulled out her Seiberling scrapbook. Flipping through the pages, she pulled out old pictures and letters that she and Carl had sent back and forth when they were younger. Annie fell asleep with an old photo of Carl still clutched in her hand.

Chapter 17
"Be a Man"

Carl's Story:

With the sun bidding its final farewells, Carl blew in through his front door like a mighty wind blows across an open field..

Once inside, Carl found his father sitting at the kitchen table with a cigarette in one hand and a cold beer in the other. Having recently retired, Mr. Ericsson went from working grueling thirteen-hour days of "pounding the pavement," as he called for six hours a day.

It's true that Mr. Ericsson gave up drinking in a manner of speaking. After the beating he inflicted upon Carl, Mr. Ericson had no choice but to accept his wife's plea-bargain agreement. Arthur substituted his taste for hard liquor to something smoother and subtler: beer. The only problem with that arrangement was that Arthur would crack open a can of America's favorite beer, "Schlitz, and begin his drinking binge from the time came home at noon until he went to bed at 8:00 p.m.

Already "three sheets to the wind," when Carl came blowing through the door, Mr. Ericsson was in his typical fashion and in true form. His body took on its normal pose for the camera; slouched in a kitchen chair with his right arm braced on the kitchen table for support and his left eye now completely shut while he fought so desperately hard to keep the right one open.

Carl hoped to escape both his father's glare and the line of questions soon to follow. But there was no other avenue or short cut through the house. Carl knew. He just knew. He witnessed it time to time with his older brothers. His father was going to batter him with ugly, degrading, verbal assaults on every front. And Carl was not disappointed either.

The moment Arthur spied his son, the denigration began."

"Where have you been boy?" Arthur slurred.

"At a friend's house." Carl respectfully answered.

Struggling to complete his sentence, Arthur still slurred: "Your twin tells me you have a girlfriend! Is that true, boy?"

Carl tried to evade and avoid his father's question. It was not that he was ashamed of Annie, by any means. Carl knew that if he truthfully answered the question, then his manhood would come under fire. In his father's eyes, at least the one that slightly remained opened, his sons were not true Ericsson's unless they were pugilistic and promiscuous.

"She is just a friend, dad." Carl answered. Like Old Faithful, his father spewed out the question he was notorious and known for.

"Well, son! Did you?" Arthur demanded. "Well, boy, did you finally become a man?"

Annoyed with his father, Carl started to show signs of frustration. What little respect he had for his father evaporated like water boiling in a hot kettle. "If it is what I think it is: then: 'No, dad! I did not.'"

Carl rattled his father's cage. Not only was Arthur agitated by his son's answer; he was angered by his son's disrespect. Arthur was true to form as he shot back: "And you call yourself a man. You will never be an Ericsson until you do it, boy. Get away from me! You make me sick."

Standing up to his father was something Carl and his brother's learned not to do. But, then again, love has a way of making people do things a person would not necessarily do. Carl stared at his father with such force, that even Arthur, despite his stupor, was somewhat taken aback.

"Are we finished, father?" Carl asked. Arthur sat silent. He sat there smiling. That was Arthur for you. He succeeded in getting under Carl's skin. However, Carl was about to push the envelope a little too close to the edge. He looked at his father one more time only to firmly say: "Sir, I just asked you a question! I believe it deserves an answer!"

Carl just did something that the other cubs from Arthur's den dared never to do. He challenged the king of his father's jungle. Carl had rattled his dad's pride. In a fit of rage, Arthur went to strike back, but he was intoxicated. As he started to rise from his seat, he fell back. Carl came very close to suffering the same fate he did some years ago.

In an attempt to regain whatever alpha male control he had over the household, Arthur blurted out something that would eventually stun Carl. The comment opened a door to a nightmare Carl had long since forgotten. "Get out of my face, boy!" Arthur commanded. "Get out of my face, boy, before I get my slapstick out and beat you silly again!"

Heading up the stairs, Carl shot back at his dad: "It will be my pleasure, old man." Grabbing clean clothes and heading off to the shower, Carl had a flashback. His mind traveled back in time. Consumed by an eerie feeling, he remembered that something terrible took place in his bathroom after a drunken interrogation from his father. As much as he tried to finish unlocking the door his father just opened, Carl's mind would not allow it.

Annie Story:

Annie took extra long getting ready for school the next morning. She wanted to look exceptionally nice for Carl. And as Annie was getting ready, she couldn't decide if she wanted to call Carl to meet and walk to school together or not. Annie knew that she did not want to be smothered by a boyfriend taking up all her free time. Annie had other friends that she liked to run around with; some of those friends were boys. Annie wondered how Carl would react if boys just happened to stop by the house and talk on the porch steps. She had male friends that she would go fishing with down at the Metro park.

She could not bear the thought of giving up her friends. She hoped Carl would be mature enough to accept that she was not going to drop all of her friends to spend all her free time with him: though they were an official couple, Annie had a life too. *"Besides, Carl has his friends and his brothers. He will want to spend time doing boy things."* Annie thought about the things boys like to do; especially with girls. *"I hope Carl isn't too pushy. I am certainly not ready for THAT!"* Annie thought.

She decided not to call Carl, but decided if she saw him along the way to walk to school with him. Annie didn't mind walking alone. Being a quiet person, she often kept to herself. She was not one for talking about what was on her mind. Annie often had a hard time conveying what she was thinking or how to say it. If something was on Annie's mind, it usually just stayed there.

Nearing the school, Annie gazed around looking for signs of Carl. Not wanting to seem desperate, Annie wasn't sure if she should wait on the stairs. She didn't' want to come across as anxious. All her composure would soon go out the window. Hearing Carl's voice behind her, she turned around throwing her arms up in the air and shouted "Carl! I've been waiting here FOREVER!" She could not contain the smile spreading across her face. Carl flashed a smile back to Annie. His smile sent a chill down her spine.

Carl's Story:

Carl showered and went straight to bed. His father's words haunted him. "Did you finally become a man?" Carl understood exactly what his father alluded to. He had heard that expression time and time again when his older brothers brought any girl to the house.

In Arthur's eyes, his son's were not men until they became sexually active. *"Did I become a man with her?"* Just as a scratch on a vinyl record had the potential to repeat the same lyrics over and over again, those words continued to replay themselves throughout Carl's evening.

Carl loved Annie. If she only knew how much he loved her. He purposed it in his mind to protect her purity; but how? *"I can't bring her home. My dad would literally drill us."* Carl's thoughts got the best of him. He screamed out: "I can't. I just can't!"

Carl and Allen shared the same room. Allen happened to enter their bedroom only to hear his twin think aloud: "You can't what?"

"Nothing!" Carl said softly weeping.

"Man." Allen teased. "Are you still crying over a girl? Dad is right, you are such a wimp."

"You don't want me to get out of my bed, do you? If you think that punch on the bridge hurt, then keep it up. I will show you what pain really is."

Allen rubbed the bruise Carl had left behind subsequent to the bridge. "Man, you do what you think you need to do. I'm out." Allen responded.

That evening crawled across the evening like a turtle crossing the expressway. Time crept while Carl's mind was bombarded with traffic. *"But how?"* He kept asking.

The light bulb finally clicked as the sun was making its presence known.

"I will protect Annie by breaking it off with her. That way, she will not have to meet my dad. I will be her Life saver." Carl reasoned. Carl rolled out bed and got ready for school.

"Are you coming with me?" Allen inquired.

"Yeah, but I still need some time to myself." Carl said. "Go on without me and I'll catch up."

"Come on, man!" Allen shouted. "Get over it!" Allen looked at his twin. He sensed Carl's anguish. "Okay, brother. I hope you work it out before you get to school." He said, somewhat sympathetically.

But Carl could not work it out. He did not want to break up with Annie. He was haunted by the question: *"But how? I can't see my life without her. But, how?"* His conclusion was the same as it was when the bolt of lighting struck some hours ago. *"I will break it off with her."* The question now evolved around on how to go about ending their relationship.

Carl finally made it to that steep concrete stairway that led to the school. His heart broke as he took each step upward. He immediately spotted Annie and was greeted with a smile and Annie's words: "Carl! I've been waiting FOREVER!" Carl was gracious enough to reciprocate a smile for a smile.

"Annie." Carl's said with a trembling voice. "Can we talk?"

"About what?" Annie reluctantly asked. "Carl, what's wrong?" Annie's female intuition and instincts went into high gear. "Carl!" She demanded. "What's going on?"

"Let's get away from everybody." Carl spoke softly. "We can go up to the cafeteria to talk." Carl took Annie's hand. They entered the school, walked up one flight of steps, and headed to the lunchroom.

They could hear an argument brewing as Allen was debating politics with other students. As luck would have it, Carl and Annie walked in at a bad time. Mike, the former Seiberling bully, decided to stand on his soapbox. Allen was already outnumbered three to one. Carl did not like the odds. And besides, Carl and his brothers were taught if someone messes with one Ericsson, then he has to deal with all of them.

But there was something more at play than the "Ericsson Code of Conduct." There was something about Mike. Though Carl could not exactly put his finger on it, Mike struck the chord on Carl's already fragile strings.

"Shut up and butt out!" Carl demanded.

"Why don't you try and make me!" Mike shot back. Those were words that Mike would eventually come to eat.

Carl politely let loose of Annie's hand. Walking up to Mike and without warning, but with much provocation, Carl made a fist and swung. He hit Mike so hard, that Mike, fell to the cafeteria floor.

The chatter in the room stopped. Mike sat on the floor holding his left jaw. He did something that shocked everyone. He cried. Mr. Griffin, an eighth-grade teacher responsible for overseeing the cafeteria, quickly whisked Carl to the office.

For some strange reason, Carl seemed to get into trouble. And for some odd reason he was getting use to teacher's escorting him to the office. There he sat once again waiting for his future. The Assistant Principal called Carl into his office, where Carl was read the riot act. He then called Carl's house where Mr. Ericsson answered the phone, of course.

The Assistant Principal explained to Carl's father about Carl's bout with Mike. He went on to explain how Carl would receive a three-day suspension. Unbelievably, the Assistant Principle started to laugh. He put his hand over the phone and asked Carl: "Your dad wants to know if you won?"

"Yes. You can tell my father, I won." Carl said with a mumble. "And sir, please let him know I knocked my opponent out with one punch."

The Assistant Principal placed the phone to his ear and said: "Mr. Ericsson, Carl won. In fact, it was not much of a fight. He used one blow to send the opposing party to the floor."

Carl could hear his father laugh on the other end of the phone. "That's my boy! You can send him home. Carl was beside himself. He couldn't believe it! The Assistant Principal read Carl the riot act, yet he received a reward from the other end of the phone. He was issued his suspension papers and freed to go.

Annie's Story:

Annie's jaw hit the floor as she watched the mayhem unfurl before her. Annie's heart raced as she stood there with her knees going weak. Grabbing Annie by her wrist, Allen pulled her across the cafeteria, down the stairs, and out the doors of the school.

Annie yelled and carried on the entire way. "Oww, you're hurting me Allen. Let me go!" Annie wailed. Annie tried to free herself from Allen's grasp, but he just squeezed harder.

"Where are we going? I can't ditch school. Allen please stop it!" Annie continued.

"For heaven's sake! Annie shut up!" Allen yelled. "We're not ditching, I just need to talk to you. You'll be back by the end of homeroom."

Rubbing her wrist where Allen had just let go, she examined the rug burn he left behind.

"How am I going to explain that?" Annie wondered to herself.

Allen and Annie walked around the side of the school, and sat on the steps in front of the library. Allen disclosed to Annie, one of the Ericsson family secrets. This secret was the reason Carl was sent to New Jersey.

Annie sat on the steps with her knees pulled into her chest. She cried into her lap as Allen told her the story. Annie wished Carl were there with her. She wanted to be with him more than ever. Her heart was breaking for him.

Allen scooted closer to Annie. Hoping to offer her some comfort, he put his arm around her. He fished around in his pocket and then pulled something out. "Annie, this will make you feel better." He said as he nudged Annie with his shoulder.

Annie took the bandana from Allen's hand and dabbed at her eyes then blew her nose. Cupping Annie's chin in his hand, Allen turned Annie's face towards him and said: "Annie, don't cry."

Carl was going to dump you today anyhow." Allen wrapped his other arm around pinning Annie down against the steps and kissed her; a hard and sloppy kiss.

Annie struggled to break free. "You better get back to school." Allen snapped as he got up. He took off running and Annie sat there, speechless. Tears flowed. Annie was completely lost. Burying her face into her lap she bawled.

Annie didn't know how much time had passed, but the flashing of red and blue lights caught her attention. "Whoop-whoop" she heard two short blasts of a police siren. A cop car stopped in front of the library where Annie sat on the steps.

An officer got out of the car. Walking towards Annie, he asked: Shouldn't you be in school young lady?"

Panic struck Annie as she thought about the trouble she was in when she got home.

"My boyfriend dumped me," Annie cried out to the officer. A thought flashed through Annie's mind, *"I know that's why Carl threw that punch at Mike; to get out of having to see me today."*

Annie was lost in thought and the officer could see that Annie was truly in distress. With empathy, the officer told her, "Let me give you a piece of advice. Put books before boys. You will get your heart broken more than once. Boys are not worth a hill of beans until they are old enough to support a wife and a family. You get yourself an education and then you worry about boys."

"I'm going to let you off with a warning." The officer said. "I expect you to get back to school and don't let boys come between you and your education."

Annie thanked him for not calling her parents. She headed back towards the school and deliberated about how she wanted to handle everything that had just happened.

"Carl is going to be so upset when he finds out about Allen and that kiss. But Carl was going to break up with me – so he probably won't care. Maybe I'll go after Allen and

make Carl jealous. I don't know what to do." Annie had so many things running through her head. *"Should I call Carl when I get home tonight?"*

Feeling overwhelmed, Annie started crying again. As she entered back into the school she saw Coach Garret, her track and field coach. He was standing in the hall.

"Annie, Annie, what's wrong? Are you alright? Here, come with me." He said, taking her through the gym and into his office. Motioning for Annie to sit, Annie sat and Coach Garret took his seat behind his desk.

Annie didn't know how much detail to dish out, but she didn't want to bring up Carl's name. She feared that it might get him or his family into trouble. But dish she did; starting all the way back in second grade, Annie began to tell her tale.

Moving from his seat to the edge of his desk, he looked Annie in the face and told her that she had a talent on the track that needed to be nurtured. "Annie, I encourage you to forget about boys." He said. "Your potential for running will get you a full ride to college one day."

The bell rang, signaling the end of a period. Annie's coach wrote her a free pass to class and she headed out of the gym.

Annie needed to get to study hall and find Jill. Jill's eyes grew as big as saucers and her mouth opened wide as Annie relayed the events of the morning.

"Annie, you are too good for Carl. Forget about him." She said.

"I can't Jill." Annie replied somberly. "I will absolutely die without him."

Allen slid into the seat behind Annie, "Annie, I'm sorry about this morning. I feel bad about what I did to you. Let's just pretend it never happened."

Annie didn't acknowledge Allen. She put her head on the desk and closed her eyes.

Annie could not wait for the day to end. She needed to run. She was looking forward to track practice after school. She needed to get her mind off Carl. The track was what she needed. Walking home after practice, Annie paused on the railroad bridge. She wondered how Carl could profess his love, tell her dad that he was going to marry her, and then promise he would never let her go, and now this mess. *Books before boys, Annie:books before boys.*

Chapter 18
"If You Are Going To Fight A Man,
You Better Fight Like One!"

Carl's Story:

Carl took his time as he walked home. His heart literally ached as he thought about Annie. He sobbed from the time he exited the school to the time he entered his home.

Arthur started his daily ritual earlier than usual. He was half-crocked by the time Carl made it home. He just sat there like a statue staring out the kitchen window. After he retired, Arthur practiced the art of feeding the local neighborhood birds. He enjoyed them as he sat on the throne of his kingdom. If, by chance, there was anything to impede the birds from eating the feed Arthur dished to them, he had a way of rectifying the problem. He took his shotgun nestled against the kitchen cabinet only to eliminate the competition. Many inner-city rats fell prey along with an occasional cat here and there to Arthur's aim.

As a matter of fact, it was not uncommon for Arthur to set his sights on things other than rodents or an occasional cat. Anytime the streets showed signs of a scuffle of some sort, he was known to grab his trusted shotgun only to stand on his front porch. With a cigarette in one hand

and his equalizer in the other, he stared up and down his street to single out his next casualty. It made no difference to Arthur. Whether he shot a rat, a cat, or some gang member, they were all the same to him.

It did not take long for everyone to take notice. It did not take long for everyone to fear him. Living a life on the streets, they very well understood he meant business. It was evident in his eyes and it was enforced by his words.

Carl tried to avoid any contact or conversation with his dad. Arthur seemed content.

But he caught sight of Carl out of the corner of his eye and the silence snapped.

"So boy, you got in another fight!" The interrogation started.

"Yes, dad! I got in another fight!" Carl blurted out. He was not in the mood to speak with his father: especially when his father was drunk.

"Boy, did you win?" Arthur demanded to know.

"Yes, dad! I did what Ericsson's do best. Aren't you proud of your son now?"

Though Arthur's mind teetered on the borders of sobriety and a drunken stupor, he sensed two things: his son's sarcasm and that his son had been sobbing.

"If you won boy, then why have you been crying?" Arthur bellowed.

"Even if I told you, you wouldn't understand." Carl replied.

Arthur mocked his son. "It's that girl, isn't it? You are crying over a girl. Girls are a dime a dozen. They are only good for one thing boy, and you are not even man enough to prove it!"

Carl stood up to his father and shot back, "What do you know about being a man? You are nothing but a deadbeat drunk. You are an old man who wasted his life drinking whiskey!"

Carl pushed one too many buttons this time. Arthur rose from the table and headed toward his son. "Oh yeah! Do you think you are man enough to beat this old man? Go ahead son, hit me." There was a long pause. "Go ahead boy! I instructed you to hit me!"

Carl started to cry. "Boy, you are nothing but a baby! You will never be a man. You are an embarrassment to the Ericsson name. Get out of my face!" Arthur sneered.

With that, Carl tightly clinched his right hand. He looked his father in the eyes and said: "That's what you think." He punched his father on the left side of his cheek. He hit his father so hard his dentures went flying across the room. Arthur snapped his head to the right and then forward. Arthur used his left forearm to wipe away the red liquid that spewed from his mouth. He was remarkably impressed as he grinned at his son.

"Not bad, my boy! But it was not good enough! If you are going to fight a man, then you better learn to fight like one." Arthur shouted. Without warning, he raised his right hand. With a tomahawk blow, he struck Carl in the head. Carl fell to the floor.

Carl knew he was beat. He did not have the strength to stand to his feet. All he could do was crawl into his room. All he could do was cry.

"That's right boy!" Arthur laughed. "Go to your room. You are a baby. And stay there! I don't want to see your sorry face again."

Carl's world was crashing down on him. He lost the love of his life and almost his life. What else could go wrong that day? Carl mustered enough strength to slowly creep to his room and to climb in bed. He buried his head in his pillow and let it all out. There was no end to his tears.

Allen eventually came home from school. Even Allen recognized something terrible happened. Trace evidence of that afternoon's confrontation could still be seen on the floor. Allen looked over only to see his father passed out.

"Carl" He thought. "Crap!" Allen ran to their room where he found Carl with his head sunk deep between his pillows. He, like his father, was passed out. Allen shook him. When Carl lifted his head, Allen was aghast at what he saw. The left side of Carl's face was swollen. Carl tried to speak, but he suffered and sustained a broken jaw from his father's blow.

"My gosh, Carl!" Allen exclaimed. "What on God's green earth happened here today?"

It was difficult for Carl to speak. He softly mumbled to his brother, "If I write a letter to Annie, could you give it to her?"

"Of course I will brother. I need to tell mom what dad did to you." He said.

Carl shook his head. He did not want his mother to know. He did not want anyone to know. He just wanted to stay in his room. He wanted to be alone. Carl knew he was beat. There was no end to his father's madness.

Allen fetched a piece of paper and a pen for Carl to script his letter to Annie. He also managed to find an envelope to place the letter in.

Carl wrote:

"To my Dearest Annie. I loved you from the moment I first saw you. I love everything about you. I love the color and the smell of your hair, your eyes with a touch of hazel. I loved how your smile seemed to make all of my problems go away."

"How could I forget about our first kiss? Do you remember? Your face was smothered in mud. I did not care. All I could do was think about you. I wanted you to know how much I cared for you."

"I am so sorry about this morning. I wish I could explain everything to you, but words do escape me. All I ask is for you to forgive me for the mess I made. I feel like there is nothing I can do right anymore. Please, I beg you: forgive me."

"Love Carl."

"P. S. Annie, you were and will always be my Lifesaver."

With his hands shaking, Carl folded the piece of paper the best he could. His eyes sobbed. His heart broke. Allen helped him place the letter in an envelope. He looked at Allen and slurred: "Will you make sure Annie gets this?"

Allen agreed. He felt sorry for his twin-brother. Allen wanted to strike back at his father. His mind was suddenly changed when their father started his regular routine of verbally bashing his boys. Looking at what happened to Carl also help sway his decision to retaliate.

Handing-off his letter to Allen, Carl went back to sleep. He ignored his mother's pleas to join the family for dinner. Arthur was completely oblivious as to what happened earlier that morning. Marie had no clue that Carl was suspended or that he sustained a striking blow from his father. Allen covered his father's crime by scrubbing the kitchen floor. Covering his father's crimes would be a burden that for Allen, would continue to get heavier and heavier.

Chapter 19
"Special Delivery"

Carl's Story:

Shortly after Arthur retired, Marie found a job working for a local dental lab. She woke up that morning and noticed Carl was not out of bed at his usual time. Though she did not think much about it, she did yell: "Carl, do you want a ride to school this morning?"

Allen answered for him. "No mom, me and Carl are walking today!"

"Okay." She answered and then proceeded to leave.

With his head still face down, Carl sputtered: "Please don't forget Annie's letter."

"I won't. I will give it to her before homeroom. I promise."

"Thanks. Let me know what she says." Carl pleaded.

"Don't you worry brother, I will." Allen said reassuring Carl.

He finished dressing and told Carl that he would see him later.

Allen walked to school. His conscience ate at him for kissing Annie. He betrayed his blood brother. He attempted to find every possible excuse under the sun only to conclude: *"I am an Ericsson. That's what Ericsson's do."* But even that served as a poor excuse.

He climbed the steep steps that led to the prison yard where he found Annie standing on the stairs with Jill. She seemed sad. Allen cautiously approached her and commented: "Special Delivery." He reached deep in his pockets and handed Annie the envelope.

She just stared at it. When she saw Carl's handwriting on it, she shoved it in the front cover of one of her books.

"Aren't you going to read it?" Allen inquired.

Still fuming over the events from the previous day, she looked at Allen only to say: "Like it's going to make any difference." She acted like nothing ever happened.

Allen stood shocked. But he was not in any position to stand up for his twin. How could he? His actions on the library steps the day before were considered by most: "unbecoming of a brother."

"What was he going to tell Carl?" He thought. *"How will Carl react to know that Annie snuffed him out?"* Allen became extremely perplexed. He stalked Annie around the halls in between every class. Every time, he asked her the same question: "Did you read Carl's letter?"

And every time he received the same answer. Annie pulled the sealed envelope from her book and yelled out: "Nope!"

The clouds that darkened the skies the day on the bridge were nothing compared to the clouds that would soon blanket Carl's soul. All day he stayed in bed. He dared not leave his room in fear of retaliation. His only thoughts centered on Annie. He prayed that she would read his letter. He prayed for them to get together. Unfortunately for Carl, God's hotline was busy that day.

The end of the school day finally arrived. Allen did not know what to do or say to convince Annie to read the letter. He did not want to face Carl. He did not really want to look at Carl's face either. Overnight, the bruising and swelling worsened. Carl looked like a truck hit him a time or two.

But Allen made a promise to his twin and a promise he kept. He came home. Slowly, he opened the door to their bedroom. Carl, though lying on his side, was wide-awake. He rolled over and looked at Allen. "Well?" Carl struggled to ask. "Did you give Annie my note?" He struggled to say.

For a brother known to be a brawler, Allen felt for his brother. "Yes, Carl. Yes, I did."

"Did she read it?" Carl asked.

"No, no she didn't." Allen said sympathetically. Allen knew he had to come clean. He started to tear-up as he confessed: "Carl, I am so sorry brother. It's all my fault."

"How is it your fault?" Carl responded.

"Brother, I didn't mean for it to happen." Allen pleaded. "But yesterday, I told Annie you planned to break up with her."

"What!" Carl tried to shout.

"That's not all. After I told her..." Allen paused. "I..." He could not complete his sentence.

"You what?" Carl yelped. "You kissed her, didn't you?" Carl struggled to ask.

"Yes, yes, I did. I am sorry Carl. Had I known dad was going to knock the snot out of you, maybe it wouldn't have happened." Allen tried to reason.

Carl rolled back over. He refused to say anymore to his twin. Life was not worth living if he could not have his Annie.

Chapter 20
"Oh Carl! If You Only Knew!"

Annie's Story:

Annie was glad that Carl was suspended. She wanted a few days to gather her thoughts before she came face to face with him in class on Monday. Annie needed to tell Carl about Allen. More importantly, she needed to talk to Allen before she spoke with Carl.

Allen bugged Annie all day to read the letter from Carl. *"He sure is persistent."* Annie thought. But Annie did not want to give Allen the satisfaction. She had an uneasy feeling about him. On her way out of school, Annie tucked the letter in her gym bag. "Books before boys Donaldson," Coach yelled to Annie as she laced up her shoes.

"I'm done with boys." Annie said to herself. Carl had hurt her for the last time.

Track practice ended and Annie started the long walk home; alone. She hated that feeling of being alone. *"It's not supposed to be like this."* She thought. Daydreaming her way home, Annie thought about the ageless love stories with Romeo and Juliet, Cleopatra and Mark Antony, Rhett and Scarlett. Annie wanted her fairy tale. She wanted the Bergman / Bogart love story. She wanted it to be with Carl.

Annie stopped on the bridge and watched a train zip by. She wondered: *"I wish I were on that train to nowhere."* Annie quickly tore through her gym bag looking for Carl's letter. *"I can't get on that train."* Annie reasoned. *"But I can send Carl's letter far from here."*

Annie dangled the envelope over the rail and was about to let it go, when she heard "Hey Wingfoot."

Startled, Annie turned around to see one of the girls from the track team. "Whatcha got there?" She asked, grabbing the letter out of Annie's hand. "Why ain't you opened it girl?" She teased.

"Because it's bad news." Annie replied.

With a twinkle in her eye, Annie's track friend said, "You want me to open it girl?"

"Go ahead." Annie replied.

After reading the letter, Annie's friend waved the letter in the air. With a grin on her face, she asked "Annie girl, who Carl? He in love with you girl."

She handed the letter back to Annie and continued on her way. Annie sat down on the edge of the bridge rail and read Carl's letter. She cried. She laughed. She shook her head. *"Did he really bring up Lifesavers?"*

The words on the letter smeared as Annie's tears dripped onto the paper. "Oh Carl, if you only knew." She cried.

Annie made up her mind to talk with Allen in the morning and to forewarn him how she planned to tell Carl about the incident on the library steps. Annie didn't want to create trouble between the brothers: she knew secrets never stay buried and Carl needed to hear it from her.

The walk home became even lonelier. *"Why do things always have to be so complicated?"* Annie wondered. She hurried home so she could make it to Catechism class at church. Annie needed divine intervention.

Annie laid her troubles at the foot of the cross that night in the church. She knew she needed to catch Allen if she wanted to see Carl before Monday. Annie went to bed feeling hopeful.

Chapter 21
"I Love You Annie Donaldson"

Carl's Story:

The evening finally settled in. The house was silent. Carl got up and headed to the bathroom. When he opened its door, everything he blocked for the past two years started to rush back to him. His mind tried so desperately to unlock the secrets that haunted him for so long: but all it allowed to unleash was his father busting through the bathroom door with a "slap stick." Everything from that point was still a blur.

He dismissed the horror of that image only to redirect it to Annie. He could not handle the thought of losing her. He started to hyperventilate. He felt smothered. The ocean started to open up. Carl stood in its waking path as those memories of days gone tried to resurface. Carl believed he was the only one standing on the beach.

Every emotion Carl ever felt, past and present, ripped through him like a person rips a piece of paper: anger, guilt, regret, rejection, and failure all came swishing down like a mighty tidal wave. The bathroom walls were closing in on him. He had to get out of there. He had to leave.

His instincts to survive kicked in. He ran to his room and grabbed whatever clothes he could find.

Allen woke up. "What are you doing?" He asked.

"Nothing. Go back to sleep." Carl muttered. Allen still caught somewhat between two worlds obliged.

Carl headed into the kitchen where he found the keys to his father's pride and joy. It was his car. As a retirement gift to himself, Carl's dad bought the car of his dreams: a black Cadillac: "Black Beauty." It had all the bells and whistles for its time. Whether Carl deliberately chose his father's car over his mother's is still a mystery to this day.

He ran outside, opened the driver's side door, put the keys in the ignition and started the car. Sure Carl had some driving skills. But they only amounted to moving cars in and out of the driveway. However, he never honestly drove a car.

He turned the headlights on, put the car in reverse and backed "Black Beauty" out of the drive. Where he was going, he did not know, but he pointed the car towards the top of his street. Cresting the hill, he made a right and weaved through the back streets. *"The expressway."* He thought. *"I will get on the expressway!"* As he rolled down Goodyear Boulevard, he half-heartedly chuckled as he drove over the bridge where he and Annie kissed. *"If Annie could only see me now!"* He thought.

At the bottom of Goodyear Boulevard, Carl turned towards Market Street. He could see the lights of the Goodyear Junior High School twinkling on top of the hill and the pond to his left as he drove by. Before making his way to the expressway, Carl made a sharp right into the school parking lot. His inexperience behind the steering wheel of a car showed.

He inadvertently made a sharp right turn into the school's driveway. As a result, he ran his father's "Black Beauty" against the guardrail gouging the passenger side. The sound of metal crunching against metal brought joy to Carl!

"Take that, you old man!" He cheerfully thought. Once on top of the hill, Carl parked the car. He reached over to his father's glove box and grabbed a marker his father used for work. He raced to the doors of the school and wrote on every window of every door: *"I Love You, Annie Donaldson!"*

When he was finished tagging doors, Carl returned to the helm. He smiled as he thought: *"Annie Donaldson, if this does not prove my love for you, I don't know what will."*

With his heart still racing 200 M.P.H., and his veins still pumping adrenaline, Carl set his sights on the expressway. "There is no stopping me!" He triumphantly blurted. Well, what he did not know was his father's car was badly injured. It required immediate medical attention. That became pretty evident as Carl drove "Black Beauty down the hill.

He heard the passenger tire scrape against the wheel well. "Crap!" Yes, reality started to set in. Carl realized he committed another immortal sin. He just broke the leg of his father's horse. All he could do was pray. Yet, it was that lame horse that saved Carl's life that evening. He was not ready to venture off on the expressway.

Common sense, which Carl was told he lacked, guided Carl home. The sound of the passenger tire screamed for immediate attention every time Carl turned to the right. Carl didn't really care. He did to his father's pride and joy the same thing his father did to Carl's pride and joy. He destroyed it.

God must have been on Carl's side. He made it home safely. But wait, there's more. Much to Carl's dismay, his mother awakened when Carl pulled his little stunt. She waited anxiously in the kitchen for him to return.

He struggled to get "Black Beauty" home and in the drive. He struggled even more when his mother asked quietly, yet firmly, "Where have you been?" She followed her question by: "What on God's green earth happened to your face?"

Afraid of the repercussions, Carl countered with: "I got in a fight at school. I am suspended."

His mother could not resist the temptation, but she had to know: "Did you win?"

Carl repeated the words of his father: "If you think I look bad, you should see the other guy?"

"Heaven's to Betsy Son, I sure hope so!" She said. Then asked, "Where have you been?"

"I needed some time think, mom." Carl's body trembled uncontrollably.

"It's about Annie, isn't it?" She inquired. She understood the pressure Arthur placed on his boys to be a true Ericsson's. She also understood Carl more than a person could ever imagine. Of all her children, she knew Carl better than he knew himself.

"Yes, mom. It's all about Annie. I can't get her out of my mind." Carl pleaded.

Carl poured his heart out to his mother. Calmly, she defined what Carl had yet to adequately describe. Sure, he verbalized it to Annie; he wrote in the letter Allen handed her; and he even went so far as to pen it on every window to every entrance to their school, but what he never experienced was somebody to adequately say it out loud.

Bonding with her son, Marie looked at Carl and said, "Son, you are in love. It is that plain and simple. You love Annie. Don't ever let go of that love. And don't you dare let your father make you into something you are not. Understood?"

"Thanks, Mom." Carl finally felt vindicated. His mother gave him exactly what he needed. She understood her son more than he ever realized.

"Oh, mom? There is one more thing." Carl said.

It caught her off-guard. "What's that?" She asked.

"I just wrecked dad's Cadillac." Carl shared. "I mean, I really messed it up!"

She reassured Carl by saying: "Don't worry. I will take care of it. It will be our little secret."

Carl hugged his mother and went to bed. *"Secrets!"* He thought. *"Isn't that what our family is all about: secrets."*

Arthur woke up the next morning. A person thought someone died when he tried to back his "Black Beauty" from the drive. Immediately, he heard the sound of his passenger tire rubbing against the wheel well. He put the car in park and investigated the source of the noise.

Yelling every imaginable curse word under the sun, he stormed into the house wanting to know what happened to "Black Beauty."

Marie let Arthur finish throwing out his superlatives. Calmly, she looked at him and said, "Don't you remember? Last night you went out for more beer. You had a brush in with a tree on the way home."

Arthur was flabbergasted. There was no way he could either verify or deny the story Marie shared. The last thing he recalled was Carl being sent home from school the previous day. The only person Arthur could blame was himself. In a fit of frustration, he dialed the number of the body shop.

Chapter 22
We're Going To The Chapel And
We're Going To Get...

Annie's Story:

In the morning, Annie reconciled with Allen while walking to homeroom. She gave him a hug. He gave her a pat on the head. "Annie." He said, "Wait for me after school and I will take you to Carl. Don't worry about 'the kiss,' I already told him." He added.

After school, she tagged along behind Allen in silence. As they reached the Ericsson house, Allen said to Annie, "My mom and dad had to take the car out for estimates." Rolling his eyes, "Don't ask. Trust me, you don't want to know. Carl is upstairs, just go on up. First door to your left."

Annie padded quietly up the stairs with her heart beating a million miles an hour. Annie poked her head in Carl's door. Lying on the bed was a motionless heap with a mop of brown hair sticking out. Annie crept across the carpet and lay down next to the crumpled heap buried deep beneath a mound of blankets. Wrapping her arm around the mound of blankets, she nuzzled her body as close as she could, and with her head on the edge of Carl's pillow, she whispered: "I'm here Carl."

Carl's Story:

Carl could not believe his ears. *"Was that, Annie?"* He raised his head as he finished his train of thought. *"It was! It was his Annie!"* His heart skipped a beat or two.

Annie's reaction was not quite what he expected though. She took one look at his face and became exceedingly petrified. Without trying to state the obvious, Annie asked: "Carl, what happened to your face?"

As if being an announcer to a Heavyweight title, Annie announced: "I was there when you punched Mike. You knocked him out in the first-round. He cried like a newborn baby. What happened since then? "

Tap dancing around the issue, "It really doesn't matter." Carl said. "What matters, is that you are here."

Carl's attempt to dodge Annie's counter failed and failed miserably. Annie threw an uppercut: "Did your father do this to you?"

"How did she know?" Carl wondered. "Annie! It's not that important. You are what is important to me. Come! Let's go!" Carl demanded.

"Where are we going?" Annie asked only to shoot back. "And don't you dare talk to me like I am a dog!"

"We don't have much time. My parents will be home soon. There's something we need to do." Carl pleaded.

"No! I am not going anywhere until I know where we are going?" Annie declared. Carl saw a side of Annie that he had never seen before. Ironically, he was impressed.

But time was working against them. Somewhat agitated, Carl countered with a right hook: "Don't you trust me? Have I ever lied to you before?"

For the first time in the bout of lovers, Carl got the upper hand. Annie just sat on the edge of his bed and quietly said: "No."

"Then we need to get moving?" Carl added.

Annie started to ask "But...?" Only to be hushed silent by Carl's finger on her mouth.

"Let's go!" He said. With that, Carl and Annie raced out of the house with their hands tightly knitted. They started to dash up Laffer Avenue. Annie had this bewildered look on her face.

Their race would suddenly come to a screeching halt as they approached the corner of Pioneer and Laffer. There stood Ed, Big Bertha's younger brother, along with his co-companion, Leroy. Both Ed and Leroy gained their fame by tormenting the neighborhood.

"Where are you two going?" Ed demanded to know. He took a look at Carl's face and asked: "Man! Who jacked you up?" Before Carl could say anything, Ed continued his line of questioning: "Aren't you an Ericsson?"

Carl, without hesitation, proudly replied: "Yes, yes, I am."

Ed knew of Arthur's reputation on the streets. Neighbors recounted how Arthur would stand on his front porch with a cigarette in one hand and a loaded shotgun in the other. He surveyed the streets when things got heated up. Some say he even set his sights on a few boys a time or two and dared them, yes, he dared them to do something.

"Man, ya dad is nuts!" Ed exclaimed. "I ain't messin with you all. Go! Man, get outta my face! And don't you dare tell ya daddy bout our run in, you hear?"

"No problem." Carl said. He then thought: *"Well, I guess it does pay to have a hillbilly for a father."*

Off he and Annie went. Where? Annie was still trying to figure out. They approached the playground behind Seiberling School. "Oh, we are going to the swings?" Annie thought. *"How romantic! That's where we shared our feelings for one another!"*

Annie was wrong. Carl had other things on his mind. She was right about one thing though. Carl was a romantic. As they dashed across the playground, interrupting football practice, mind you, all Annie could do was just watch the swing-sets slowly fade in the distance.

"Carl!" She shouted and then asked: "Where are we going?"

"We are almost there!" He said. They approached a small community church located next door to the school. Carl and Annie stopped in front of its doors.

"You brought me all the way up to church?" Annie asked. She could not believe her eyes. *"Church?"* She thought. *"I just went to church last night! Whoever hit Carl, must have knocked some screws loose?"*

Not knowing if the doors to the church were opened, Carl prayed as he reached for the handles. Much to his surprise, the doors freely flung open. What Carl believed to be Divine Providence was, in fact, pure luck. The pastor left the doors open for a board meeting that evening.

He was not sure exactly where he was going, but he escorted Annie up the stairs, hoping they led to the desired destination. Carl guessed right. For on their left, sat the sanctuary. It was silent and still. It was a somber moment.

Annie could not help but interrupt Carl's thoughts by whispering: "Why are we here?"

Carl pointed to the front of the church. "Let's go up front!" He softly said.

"For what? I went to church last night!" Annie replied.

"You will see." With that, Carl led Annie to the front pew.

"Take a seat." Carl strongly suggested. "We need to pray."

"About what?" Annie's temper started to show.

"For forgiveness." Carl added.

There, in the solitude of the sanctuary, Carl and Annie sat. There they sought for forgiveness. When Carl was finished, he looked to Annie and asked the same question he asked some times before: "Annie, will you marry me?"

Annie could not help but say: "You know my answer."

Carl then took her hand. He led her before the stain-glass windows and he made a vow. "Annie." Carl stated. "Before God Almighty, I promise to love you for the rest of my life. I promise not to do anything that may hinder you or hurt you. I promise to always protect you and keep you pure. So help me, God!"

Carl then did an encore performance as he did on the bridge. He tenderly placed his right hand on Annie's left cheek, all the while moving it to the back of her neck. Running his fingers through Annie's dark brown hair, Carl gently guided her face to his. There before God Almighty, Carl sealed his vows with a kiss.

Annie's Story:

Annie had no clue why they came to church to seek forgiveness. It made her wonder what Carl did that required forgiveness. Annie was relieved, however, to learn that Carl was a Christian. It stood to reason that if he was in church praying for forgiveness, that he indeed was a Christian.

Standing in front of the stained glass window, Annie watched the colorful sun rays beam across the floor. Carl's arms were wrapped around her waist and her head lay against his chest.

The moment was absolutely perfect. *"This is where I want to get married."* Annie thought.

She stood in the embrace daydreaming about marrying her best friend. There could not be a more perfect moment than this. Annie didn't want to let go.

"What are you kids doing in here?" A voice asked. "Go on now and go home."

Sensing that Annie was crying, "You okay?" Carl asked.

Nodding her head, "It's perfect Carl. But I need to tell you something that happened with Allen."

"I already know and it's forgiven." Carl said reassuringly. Annie gave Carl a hard squeeze and understood her reason for being in the little church.

"I need to get home Carl. My mom is going to wonder what happened to me." Annie worried.

Carl gave Annie a quick peck on the top of her head. She then turned and headed for home. Hearing a mournful train whistle in the background made Annie think back to the tracks that led to nowhere. She mouthed a 'thank you' to God for His divine intervention that kept her from dropping Carl's letter. She was at peace with everything in her life and hoped it would last.

Chapter 23
"Just Admit It: I Am An Ericsson"

Carl's Story:

Carl walked Annie across the parking lot and watched her as she crossed the street where she ran across the fields of Reservoir Park. He was in awe. *"If Annie only knew how much I love her."* He thought. *"I will marry you someday Annie Donaldson."* Carl's thought went from being a thought to an audible expression as he accidentally shouted aloud: "That's a promise!"

"What's a promise?" Allen asked. Carl was startled to see Allen standing by his side.

Concerned, Allen thought it best to check up his younger twin.

"Nothing." Carl responded. "Absolutely nothing."

"Carl, you were never good at lying. You are in love with Annie. Just admit it." Allen said assuredly. "And brother, I don't blame you. She is perfect for you!' C'mon, we need to get home before mom and dad."

Carl and Allen hustled through the schoolyard and headed towards home. Thankfully, everything was downhill from there. Inertia pulled them toward their home. Carl looked up. The beauty of that evening complimented his feelings. The dark clouds that covered his heart rolled back. Carl felt the warmth of something more powerful than the orange glow of the sun setting in the west. It was love.

With the forces of gravity pulling the twins downhill, they stumbled across Ed and Leroy still standing on the corner. They prepared to exchange fists with the two, but that was not going to be necessary. Much to their surprise, the only fists that were going to fly that evening came in the form of handshakes.

Ed and Leroy extended out their hands to Carl and Allen. The Ericsson twins reciprocated. "Whatz ya guys up too?" Ed asked.

With his jaw still discombobulated, Carl tried to laugh as he stated: "We are trying to make it home before our old man. You know how he can be."

Ed agreed: "So we hear. Geta a goin b'fore he gets ahome. Good luck."

To make ground from time lost, Carl and Allen double-timed it along the flattened plain of Laffer Avenue followed by sprinting down the rest of its hill. Their best efforts proved futile. It was too late. Their parents returned home.

They put on the brakes to their feet. "What are we going to do?" Carl said, shaking.

"Nothing." Allen said. "Don't worry Carl. We will walk in the house as if nothing happened. Dad dare not say anything with mom there."

Allen was wrong. He was dead wrong. There, Arthur sat on his throne. And he did say something. He was sober and somber over his "Black Beauty." His recollection of events was somewhat fuzzy at best. He took one look at Carl's face and asked: "Son what happened to your face?"

Carl froze in his footsteps. *"How can you forget?"* He thought angrily. But then he looked at his father's face. It was disfigured from Carl's punch. Carl laughed in front of his father. "I don't know dad, I was thinking the same thing about your face."

"Your mother tells me I must have hit my head falling." Arthur countered. "I remember you told me how you knocked that boy out in one punch."

Carl pulled a play from his father's book. "I did dad. If you think I look bad, you should see the other guy."

Unbelievably, he won his father's favor. "That's my boy!" He affirmed.

Words escaped Carl. He went to his room. Everything seemed right with the world. He made up with Annie. In fact, in his heart of hearts, he married Annie. And to add icing on the cake, he found approval from his father for fighting. Since it was too painful to smile, Carl was satisfied. *"I am an Ericsson!"*

His moment was quickly interrupted when it dawned on him the reality of what his father meant. He was becoming something contrary to the tender heart that supplied Carl's soul with a conscience. He was becoming a fighter: he was becoming like his father. "Oh Lord, please help me!" He cried to himself.

Chapter 24
"Annie's Junior High Years"

Annie's Story:

Although Annie's heart was devoted to Carl, she refused to be consumed by him. Annie wanted balance in her life and in her life with Carl. Yes, she and Carl were passionate about one another: but they also had passions uniquely their own. Annie loved Carl and Carl knew it.

Throughout their time in junior high, their educational paths rarely crossed. They each were gifted in their own ways. Carl was an academic standout, while Annie was just average. School was a struggle for her. Annie was often grounded for poor grades. She envied Carl for how easily good grades came to him.

Annie's gift was on the oval track and the cross-country course. Annie was a standout in both sports. Her athleticism was starting to catch the attention from the collegiate field. She spent a lot of time with the running crowd, while Carl kept his nose in the books.

In school, Annie's eyes lit up when she would pass Carl in the hall. When he was able, Carl waited for Annie by her locker so they could walk together to their respective classes. And without fail, every day over the three years in junior high, Annie would stuff a love letter through the vents of Carl's locker. Carl had a spirited side. Sometimes his foolishness got him in trouble, but Annie was pleased to see his temper and penchant for fighting had greatly diminished.

While Carl and Annie labored through junior high, they made sure they devoted time to one another. Annie was not allowed out on school nights, but Carl would often walk her home from school. It was not unusual for him to stick around for supper at the Donaldson's. Once in a while they would stop by Carl's to sit on his porch before finishing the walk up to Annie's house. On the porch, they spent time with Allen and his crazy antics. Sometimes Carl's dad would start spouting nonsense about what it meant to be an Ericsson. Carl and Annie took that as a signal to leave.

Carl and Annie went out as often as two young teens possibly could. The two attended school basketball games together. Carl went to all of Annie's field and cross-country events. In the summer they could be found soaking up the sun at a private swimming pool. Regardless of where they went or what they did, Annie's favorite past time was hanging out on the playground behind Seiberling School with Carl.

Annie's family thought the world of Carl; and so did Annie.

Chapter 25
"Who Says Leopards Can't Change Spots"

Carl's Story:

Carl changed. Whether it was his and Annie's experience in the church or the realization that Carl was no different than his father, it was hard to say. Both events had a profound effect on Carl. He knew that night something had to change: he was that something.

The handwriting was on the wall. If Carl did nothing to better his lot in life or get a firm handle on the temper that had a handle on him, more than likely, he stood a good chance of loosing Annie. Carl clearly understood Annie's deepest admiration for him, but even that affection could only go so far. He went before the threshold of grace for a second time. He pleaded with the most Holy of Holies to cleanse his heart and to make him a new creature.

He made a second vow within hours of his first. He vowed to follow in the footsteps of Christ. He promised to change his life covered with spots from the past. Though Carl did not completely understand the full extent of his petitions, he did know this: he loved Annie. He knew that had he not changed his spots, he would be on the verge of losing the best thing that ever happened to him.

Whereas God's hotline seemed so preoccupied days prior, Carl's prayer made it through without incident. Something miraculous took place: something beyond reason; and something beyond any kind of rationale. For the first time, Carl experienced a love so great that it completely enveloped him. He truly felt the power of forgiveness. He truly felt the power and presence of a Father far greater than the one who reigned from the kitchen table. It was as the "Good Book" declares: "A peace that passed all understanding."

Carl was finally at peace. He was in the presence of peace. That evening he slept like he never slept before. When morning rolled around, Carl was prepared to face the consequences for defacing every entrance door to the school by writing "I Love You Annie Donaldson!" But there was no amount of punishment the school could possibly mete out to make Carl regret for so openly and freely expressing how he felt. Besides, it was well protected under the First Amendment giving and granting all people the freedom of speech.

Ironically, school officials never did discover the culprit. They had suspicions, but that's all they had.

Carl reported to the office as instructed. His mother was finally informed of Carl's three-day pass. She took the time to drive him to school that day. She wanted to know how the system responsible for educating its students, but also providing a safe environment for such learning, could allow her son to take such a beating.

Marie literally stood in a state of shock when the school explained that Carl was not seriously injured. In fact, they recounted the event as it made its way among the student body. "It was not much of a fight at all." The Assistant Principal said. "From what we gathered, Carl hit Mike and Mike hit the floor."

Mrs. Ericsson had a difficult time digesting what she heard. *"Who in the world had the strength to inflict such an injury?"* She thought.

Something inside her flipped the switch. The light bulb turned on. "Arthur!" She murmured under breath. *"Now it all makes sense."* She reasoned. It could be the only answer.

Arthur, like Carl, sustained severe facial wounds at approximately the same time. She dismissed the thought of how Arthur must have stumbled over his two feet in a state of stupor. But all she had were suspicions. Because none of her son's came forward, Marie had no way to support or substantiate the obvious.

Carl, on the other hand, was excited to be among his friends. He was even more anxious to see Annie. Thinking about her brought a smile to his face. He sat in the office waiting for the school bell to ring. The office was slow in processing the required paperwork. Unfortunately for Carl, homeroom expired when the office finally released him from custody.

He headed to his locker with a free pass in hand. Much to his surprise, there was a letter dangling inside. It was from Annie. She was the first to welcome him back and the first to express her heartfelt desire to meet him before track practice.

Carl smiled. "I could get used to this." He thought. "Be careful what you wish for," as the old cliché declares. Every day for the rest of their time in school together, he received a note in his locker. Annie had a way of saying something new and affectionate every day. It was something that never got old and it was something that yielded the same reaction: chills down his spine, followed by a sheepish grin. *"You are killing me softly Annie Donaldson."*

Carl kept all of Annie's letters in a box that sat on the top shelf of his locker. He loved how Annie sprayed the letters with her perfume. He made it a practice to hold the notes close to his nose and inhale the scent. It sent Carl soaring to new heights. With tender loving care, he folded her notes where he tucked them in with the others as if he were tucking a baby to sleep. *"Annie Donaldson, I will marry you one day."* He thought. *"Even if it kills me."*

If there was one thing his parents instilled in Carl, it was to get an education. Annie became Carl's incentive to excel in his studies. He studied and he studied hard. A mediocre student at Seiberling, Carl proved he had the "right stuff" to hang with the best: that was in the field of academics.

He was fully aware of Annie's love for track and cross-country. He supported her to no end. Any time an opportunity presented itself to sit in the stands or stand in the fields to watch Annie compete, Carl was there. Proud! Yes, he was very proud of her accomplishments. Though it was in the far distant, he knew Annie was a natural.

The best way to describe her athleticism on the field would be to compare it to a deer running full stride in an open field: powerful yet graceful; effortless yet fast. It did not take spectators long to figure out who Carl came to watch. A person did not have to be a rocket scientist. Carl screamed for Annie well before the gun sounded. There were times he lost his voice cheering her on.

Most young couples would have snapped under the strain of school and sports. This was not the case for Annie and Carl. As time marched on, their love for one another became exceedingly evident to everyone. They supported one another in their endeavors, all the while, finding time to spend time with one another.

There was one hurdle Carl had yet to conquer. It was his father, Arthur. Anytime and every time Carl returned home from a date, his dad continued his interrogation tactics. He sat on his throne and asked the same question time and time again: "Well, boy! Did you prove yourself a man yet?"

Time and time again, Carl proudly snapped back: "No, sir! I did not prove my manhood yet!"

Carl would then ignore his father's bantering as he learned to leave the field of battle. He went to his room. He could hear his dad from a distance shouting out his disdain: "You are not a man until you do, boy!"

"Then, I guess I am not a man." Carl shouted back. He countered his rhetoric's by thinking: *"A person is defined by his character, not his conquests over women."*

Outside of his manhood constantly being challenged by his father, the secrets of the Ericsson home remained buried deep within the still waters. But even water has its boiling point: particularly when it is left on the hot surface of a stove. And beneath the murky waters of the Ericsson home, the pilot light was starting to get hot.

Chapter 26
"Welcome to High School Annie"

Annie's Story:

Annie could not wait to be an East High Oriental. High school meant Annie was closer to realizing her dreams. Annie knew two things for certain. She would go to college to become a secondary education teacher – and then she would become Mrs. Carl Ericcson.

Annie had much to be thankful for. She and Carl endured junior high and were still very much in love with one another. There were always boys asking Annie out, but her answer was always "No." Annie was never tempted to stray. She was true to Carl.

They both had large circles of friends that they spent time apart with. In high school, Annie would not have classes together with Carl. It made her sad that she never got to sit next to him in school, but Carl's academic course work was way out of Annie's league. On the other hand, Carl knew never to challenge Annie to a race.

Annie and Allen were in several classes together. She enjoyed the camaraderie they had built together. After all, it was Allen who brought her and Carl back together. Besides, Annie knew that Carl was very close to his twin and Annie felt that having Allen near was the next best thing. Carl made a point to be standing at her locker every day after school. They say old habits die-hard. Annie continued to barrage Carl's locker with her love letters on a daily basis.

In their junior year, Carl and Annie started discussing plans for after graduation. Scouts had their eye on Annie, who had broken several school and citywide track and field records. She was a shoe-in for a full ride to a college of her choice. Annie realized that their career paths would take them in opposite directions after graduation, but that was two years away and she didn't' want to think about it.

Midway into their junior year, Annie had a schedule change which allowed her to have lunch with Carl. Annie was happy about that. She loved being able to see Carl in the middle of the school day. When Carl acquired his driver's license, he drove Annie home after school on the nights she didn't have practice.

Sometimes Carl and Annie would stop at the little church next to Seiberling School. There the two would spend some quiet time sitting silently in the sanctuary.. Sometimes their moment was broken by the woeful sound of the train whistle blowing from the train at the bottom of the hill. There was something about the train bridge, the whistle, and the tracks going nowhere that beckoned Annie. Annie could never put her finger on it, but for some reason, the sound always left Annie with a melancholy feeling.

Chapter 27
"Finally!"

Carl's Story:

Finally, Carl lived long enough to make it to high school. He loved everything about the experience. The smell of the halls, the traffic of students hustling down the corridors, the local news as it spread from one student to another and from one classroom to the other. Carl finally found his place.

There was nothing he could not do. He continued to master his studies. His charisma made him one of the most popular students. Though girls tried to pry him away from Annie, he politely refused any and all invitations. In fact, many girls tempted Carl. They opened the door by enticing him to enter the Garden of Eden, where he had full rights to partake of the forbidden fruit. It was difficult for Carl to resist.

There were two consequences if he chose to accept. But those consequences were at the opposite ends of the polar continuum. On one hand, if he opted to bite from the apple, he would gain his father's approval. He would be "a man: an Ericsson" in his father's eyes. On the other hand, he stood to lose the person that mattered most: Annie.

Although the temptation presented itself time and time again, Carl remained firm and faithful to Annie.

High school loved Carl and Carl loved high school. Each year he demonstrated signs of maturing into a fine young man. No longer was he defined as a "scrapper," but rather as a model student. He gained the trust of the students, as well as the school staff. He renewed his reputation. He delved into every extra-curricular activity the school had to offer. He became actively involved in student council, the yearbook staff, the spirit committee, and the list could go on.

While Annie represented her school on the track, Carl was regarded as an ambassador for the "scarlet and gray." He accepted the position to sit on the superintendent's roundtable. Regardless of their busy schedules, Carl and Annie always made time for each other. If they were not talking on the phone in the evening, they were sending notes to one another.

On the weekends, Carl and Annie spent time together either by sitting in the Donaldson home, walking through the Goodyear Metro Park, or by sitting on the swings behind Seiberling School. As they grew into young adults, so too did the love they shared for one another. Despite his many achievements in the school, Carl's greatest accomplishment in life was winning the affection of Annie.

Chapter 28
"Prom Drama"

Time was running its course for both Carl and Annie. The spring of their junior year was on the horizon. Carl was excited because it meant their Junior Prom would be soon approaching. Carl looked with great anticipation to ask Annie's hand. What Carl was not prepared for, was her answer.

She said: "No!" Carl could not believe his ears. *"How could she say no! How dare she say no!"* Carl thought.

Annie saw the disappointment as it was written all over his face. She then explained her dream of waiting for their senior year. For Annie, the senior prom had more meaning to her. She even went so far as to say "yes." Carl was freed from asking her.

Before Annie and Carl knew it, their senior had slipped through their fingers. It seemed like yesterday when they first walked through the doors of East High School. Both were respected for their achievements, not only in the class or cross-country course, but also for their commitment to one another. While some students envied the love they shared, the majority cheered them on as Senior prom was a few weeks within Annie's reach. Yet, Carl had not asked her. She made no qualms about her desire of attending this most social and sacred event for seniors.

She dreamt about this magical event for many years. She knew with the right person, prom night would be magical; a night to remember. While Annie had experienced many magical moments with Carl, she looked forward to their Senior Prom with great anticipation. It would be the one night that she would slip into a gown and become his princess: his Cinderella. Carl knew that Annie had great expectations for that night. And Annie knew that Carl would not disappoint her.

Senior Prom also meant that graduation would soon follow. Annie didn't want to think about what would come after graduation. She was living in the moment. The East High Senior Committee had posters plastered all over the halls of the school. Annie wanted Carl to officially ask her to go with him. It didn't matter that they both already knew they were going with one another.

She dropped hints to Carl. "Don't you have something you want to ask me?" She would say to him while poking him with her finger. "Oh look Carl, a poster for Prom! What do suppose that it's advertising?" Carl was toying with her.

He waited as long as possible to pop the question. He loved it when Annie threw her little jabs here and there. Like clockwork, Annie hounded Carl every day with her subtle hints.

Carl laughed as he jokingly stated the obvious. "Yes, I see those posters. But I am not quite sure how to interpret them. Is the senior class planning something?"

Annie's patience started to run a little thin. Senior Prom was within weeks and Carl still had yet to pop the question.

Agitated, Annie shouted at him while they were eating lunch. "Are you or are you not going to ask me to the dance Carl?" All conversations ceased. Everyone looked up to see Carl's response. All eyes were on Annie and Carl.

"Well!" She demanded. "Are you or aren't you?"

All he could do was smile. "I am still thinking about it. I am not use to rejections. If I remember correctly, you said 'no' to me last year."

Adding to the drama Carl wailed out loud, "Oh!" He cried. "You didn't care about my feelings. You just said no!"

Sobbing Carl went on with his Oscar performance. "You wanted to wait for Senior Prom! Did ever consider how I felt? No!" He blurted while wiping his nose.

Annie had a enough. She bolted out of the cafeteria in tears. Everybody thought this was it. This would be the straw to break the camel's back. They were done! Well done! They were history, as a matter of speaking.

Jill stood up and put her two cents in: "Carl! You are a jerk!"

Carl sat there, still wiping the fake tears from his face. Jill was in hot pursuit of Annie. When both girls left the cafeteria, Carl stood up and counted backwards. He started with ten. He did not even make it five when Annie burst through the cafeteria doors.

"You are a jerk! Carl Ericsson. My answer is yes!"

What Annie did not know is Carl convinced some underclassmen to stand outside the cafeteria. Each one was summoned to hold up a sign. When joined together the sign read: "Annie Donaldson: May I have the honor to take you to Prom?"

The cafeteria erupted in laughter. Carl stood up and took his bow before the crowd. He placed his hands on Annie's shoulders only to say: "Clockwork, Miss Donaldson. You are like clockwork!"

Crying, Annie snapped back. "And you are still a jerk, Carl Ericsson!"

Love! That's all that needs to be said. Pure and unadulterated love!

Chapter 29
"The Proposal!"

Carl's Story:

It was prom night. This day held so much potential and promise. But life has a way of throwing a curve ball every now and then. That day, Carl received a letter of acceptance to Annapolis, the United States Naval Academy. It was something he wanted from the time he first saw a picture of his father wearing a naval uniform. It was his way of gaining his father's approval.

The entire family celebrated as Carl read the letter. Even his dad was proud of him. After their time of congratulating Carl, he and Allen had to pick up their tuxedos for the big evening.

Ironically, Allen and Jill became an item. Since his little encounter and incident with Annie, Allen and Jill formed a partnership when they successfully brought Carl and Annie back together.

They rented a limousine for this special evening. All four planned to say their final farewells to the "scarlet and gray." Carl headed straight for the bathroom to shower. He opened the door only to be greeted by an uneasy feeling.

"Something happened in here. Something quite tragic too." Carl started having flashbacks again about his father busting through the door, but that was a far as his mind would allow him to go.

He shook those memories back as there were bigger and better things in store for him. He just received his acceptance letter and prayerfully that would not be the only acceptance he received that day. He showered and put on his tuxedo.

Right as he was to leave with Allen, their dad walked up to Carl and did something out of the ordinary. "Here Son!" Arthur said, holding his car keys out to Carl. "Here are the keys to my baby. You take good care of her, you hear boy?"

Shocked, Carl said: "Yes, sir." The last time he took the helm of "Black Beauty," he rammed it into a guardrail. "Are you sure, Dad?"

"Son, I am very proud of you!" Arthur said. However, Arthur did what Arthur did best. He drank. The alcohol soon took over. It was clear by his next statement. "Now son, you are going to be a man with her, aren't you?"

Carl smiled into his father's eyes. "Dad, I promise you, I will be a man in ways you never thought possible."

"That's my boy!" Arthur said proudly.

Carl snatched the keys from his father and headed towards "Black Beauty." His mother chased after him.

"Carl!" She shouted. "You cannot forget this." She handed Carl something very precious: very valuable. It was a roll of Lifesavers.

"Thanks mom." He said, and then followed up by asking: "Is everything okay with dad?"

With a heavy heart, Carl's mom looked to the ground and cried: "No, Son. Everything is not fine with your father. He has terminal cancer."

Carl did not know what to do. Her tears became his tears. "Oh, mom." He sobbed. "What are we going to do?"

Regaining whatever composure she had, she ordered Carl: "Now son, this is what you are going to do."

"You are going to have a great evening with Annie. Do what you have to do and we will worry about your father later." Carl stood there. His entire body went numb.

"Go! Have a great time son!" Marie said for a second time. "Don't make me repeat myself."

Still crying, Carl shouted out: "Yes, ma'am."

He took the helm of his dad's "Black Beauty." Memories of that evening came racing to the lead. Carl laughed to himself when he recounted how he smashed the passenger side into the guardrail. He cried as he laughed now knowing his father was terminal.

The clock was working against him. He knew it. However, before making it to Annie's house, he had to pull over. He could not contain or restrain his emotions. Of all places, he pulled into the parking lot of that small community church.

There, he sought guidance again from the Father who reigns over all creation. "What am I am supposed to do?" He shouted.

The answer came quick and swift. The Spirit of the Most Holy of Holies whispered in Carl's ear. "Do what I have pre-ordained you to do!"

Carl understood exactly what God had just instructed him to do. He dried the tears that saturated his cheeks and he went to pick up the love of his life: Annie Donaldson.

He pulled into her driveway, exited the car, and like a member of the family, stepped in her house without knocking. He stopped dead in his tracks when he saw his Annie. She was beautiful: she was radiant. Carl could not help but stare at her.

"Oh my!" Carl could not control how he felt. "You are so beautiful!"

Mr. Donaldson quickly interrupted Carl before he said something he would later regret. "That's my daughter you are talking about."

"I know! But with all due respect dad, I may call you dad."
Carl said jokingly and then seriously. "She is stunning! Sir,
you must know how much I care for Annie!"

"Yes, son, I may call you son?" Mr. Donaldson responded.
"That's why I am trusting her into your care. You do what
you must this evening." With that, Mr. Donaldson winked
at Carl.

Mrs. Donaldson was quick to rush into the room. "You
can't go until we have some pictures. Oh look at you two!"
She said. "You make such a cute couple."

"Here!" She exclaimed. Stand in front of the fireplace so I
can get a picture of you two."

What Mrs. Donaldson said next blew Carl clean out of
the water. "Well, Carl! Just don't stand there, kiss her!"
Awkward was an understatement. But Carl did as he
was instructed. It did not bode well with Mr. Donaldson,
though.

"That was something I did not need to see." He somewhat
chuckled.

With that Carl and Annie were off to the Prom. Annie
could not wait to enter the doors. That year's theme was
based on Roberta Flack's number one hit ten years prior:
"Killing Me Softly." How appropriate for a couple whose
love stood the test of time.

Annie loved everything about the room. Her eyes lit up
as she saw the red and white streamers dance along the

ceiling. There were hearts spread on the tables. Vases with red and white roses adorned tabletops. What caught Annie's attention was the stage. She saw two chairs sitting atop the platform.

She whispered a simple prayer: "Dear Lord, I pray Carl and I are voted King and Queen." That prayer definitely would have completed Annie's fairy-tale wish. Oh, if she only knew what God had orchestrated.

Annie was so unprepared for everything that would happen that evening. Jill and Allen arrived and met up Carl and Annie. They found their seats only to spend most of the time intermingling with friends.

Students started to show off their fancy footwork as they stepped onto the dance floor. Carl and Annie were slow to accompany the other students. They waited for a slow and romantic song. They were content to fall into each other arms, look into one another's eyes, and if the mood was right, kiss.

They had to wait for that song. The principal stepped onto the stage to announce the King and Queen. The music stopped, the dancing ceased, and the room stood still.

The principal paused as he opened the envelope. He stood silent and still adding to the anticipation building among the student body. Finally, he broke the silence by stating: "This years' Prom Queen and King are...." He followed it by another long pause.

Allen, being Allen, blurted out: "Spit it out!"

The principal laughed. "Very well." He said. "This should not be surprising to most. This year's Queen and King are none other than Annie Donaldson and Carl Ericsson."

Annie was completely got off guard. Never in a million years could she imagine this moment. But her dream did come true and her prayer was answered. Cinderella's carriage finally arrived.

Carl escorted Annie to the stage where they received their crowns. The principal looked at Carl and asked: "Is there anything you would like share."

Speaking into the microphone, Carl said: "Yes, sir. Yes, there is."

Carl reached deep down into the front pocket of his tuxedo. To everybody's amazement, he pulled out a roll of Lifesavers. Yes, he pulled out a roll of Lifesavers.

Allen blurted out a second time: "What the...!"

He was never able to finish his sentence as Carl handed the Lifesavers to his Annie. She did not know what to say or what Carl was up to. No one expected what was to happen.

Coaxing Annie, "Go ahead, open it." He said.

Annie slowly started to open the roll of Lifesavers. Much to her surprise, the first Lifesaver she saw was a diamond ring. Within its inlet was a piece of paper that was precisely folded into a perfect circle.

The day that Carl requested Annie's presence to attend Prom, his mother inquired what his future plans with Annie would be. He did not have to hesitate to answer. "I want to marry Annie. I want to spend the rest of my life with her."

"When do you plan to propose?" She inquired.

"At the Prom, mom." He answered.

Not having any daughters, Marie always desired to hand-off the diamonds she received from her mother to the next generation of girls. Annie was going to be her first. Marie then shared how she would have the diamonds fitted into a ring and also shared how she would be honored to sew a wedding dress for Annie. Both mother and son cried joyfully.

Annie stood as still as a statue. Carl encouraged her: "Go ahead and read it! Please be sure to read it out loud."

Her hands shook. Could it be? Could this be the fairy-tale she dreamt of so long ago? The answer was "YES! YES! Dreams do come true."

She unfolded the letter only to read out loud to the senior class not a statement, but rather a proposal. It was hard to understand what she said as her bottom lip quivered. But most people got the gist. She struggled, but she finally found the strength: "Annie Donaldson, would you marry me?"

If Carl believed her eyes glistened when he walked through the Donaldson home some hours ago, he was wrong. He was dead wrong. Annie's eyes beamed and streamed. She looked up to him. With tears of joy, she did not hesitate to answer: "Yes, you jerk! Yes, I will marry you."

Neither Carl nor Annie sat in their respective chairs. Instead, they danced to the song that was killing them softly. How fitting! How appropriate! Love! Unadulterated and pure love!

As Carl placed his hands on Annie's waist, he answered his father's question. "Yes, Dad! Yes, I just became a man. It is something you have yet to learn! Be proud old man."

Chapter 30
"I Would Say 'Yes' To Anything"

Annie's Story:

In rhythm to the music, Annie swayed with Carl. Her head rested upon his chest and her arms draped around his shoulders. The bands of light reflecting from the diamond ring mesmerized her.

Pondering the events of the evening, Annie had responded to Carl's proposal numerous times over the course of their relationship. Not one for the spotlight, she wished for a moment of solitude. With her body pressed against his, she wished it were just the two of them. Nuzzling her face into the crook of Carl's neck, she gave him a squeeze and said: "I would say 'yes' to anything you want to ask of me tonight."

It was on this night, that Annie anticipated Carl asking her a very intimate question. Annie's Catholic upbringing taught that one should save their purity for the sanctity of marriage. Annie wanted to abide by the teaching of the Church, but she knew that there would be no one before Carl, nor would there be anyone after Carl. Annie was saving herself for Carl and Carl alone. As much as Annie wanted to wait, she also was very much in love with him. She wanted to be with Carl in the same manner that a wife is with a husband. Annie was willing to make the sacrifice. She wanted to offer Carl a definitive demonstration of how much she loved him.

"Annie," Carl whispered and gently kissed her on the forehead. "There will be a time for that." Annie didn't think it was possible, but her love for Carl deepened that night.

Chapter 31
"Till We Meet Again"

Annie's Story:

Prom night was a whirlwind. Graduation soon followed. Annie dreaded the dark period that was to follow Graduation.

Annie stood at the gate with tears streaming down her face as Carl boarded a plane to Annapolis. She wanted nothing more than to follow Carl to Maryland, but Annie's future was as a cross-country athlete at Boston College. Annie had a full ride and wanted a degree in secondary education. Annie's saving grace was that Carl was only a four-hour train ride away. Annie and Carl made plans to take the train and meet in Trenton, N.J. every few weeks. Trenton was the midway point between them and Carl had family in New Jersey that would put them up.

Carl settled in at Annapolis and a few weeks later Annie was setting down roots in Boston. What should have been a happy time for Annie was anything but. She was lonely. She ached for Carl. She missed his touch, his smile, and his scent. She longed to be wrapped in his arms. She wished that he would have said, "Yes" the night of prom.

Annie was tortured by his physical absence from her life. *"I don't want to go on without him."* While Annie longed for Carl, she found comfort in a lonesome cry of a train that whistled late into the night. It reminded her of "their bridge". Annie could never let him know how miserable she was. Annapolis was Carl's dream and she would not stand in the way.

Chapter 32
"Dashed Dreams, A Dying Dad And A Damsel In Distress"

Carl's Story:

Boarding the plane was the hardest thing Carl ever had to do. Sure, he had high hopes. His dreams were becoming a reality. He was headed for Annapolis and he was head over heels in love. What more could a young man ask?

But what Carl had yet to learn is that life is not fair. His plans to meet Annie every few weeks were null and void. He was considered a "plebe." Plebes were not permitted to leave the campus grounds except for the holidays.

Letters were often regulated and distributed at the school's discretion. Very rarely did he get a chance to read Annie's letters. He needed her encouragement. The demands placed on cadets were beyond description. Sure Carl had the aptitude and the attitude of the military. His father made sure of that. Carl was used to someone screaming in his face. He learned "how to take it like a man" as his dad use to say.

Carl's world, however, came crashing down. Right before the end of his second year, he received his stack of mail. There were two letters that broke the spirit of Carl.

The first letter came from his mother. In it, she shared with her son how bad his father was getting. The cancer was spreading throughout his body more rapidly than the oncologist had thought. Despite the several surgeries Arthur endured coupled by radiation and chemotherapy, the prognosis was dim.

His dad was dying. Carl had a difficult time digesting the news. He was angry. He wanted to make his father proud, yet Arthur would never see his son become a naval officer. More importantly, though, Carl knew he probably would never hear the four words he so desperately needed to hear from his father: "I love you, son."

"What's the point?" He thought. *"Why try anyway? I probably won't gain my father's approval or acceptance."* Carl pondered about leaving the Academy. He tried to find a reason to remain.

It was the second letter that served to be the nail that drove his decision home. It was from Annie. Carl knew in his heart of hearts that Annie would never do anything to jeopardize his dream.

She missed Carl just as much as Carl missed her. His damsel was in distress. He needed to see her, touch her, feel her, and hug her. His heart silently cried. His heart broke. His moment was interrupted as all cadets were called to the field outside the dorms.

For some odd reason, the senior cadet sensed Carl's vulnerability. Officers were not to show any signs of weakness. The senior cadet pushed one too many buttons as he continued to scream in Carl's ear. He went too far when he yelled: "What are you going to do? Cry?" He followed his demeaning spirit by adding: "Go ahead cry baby! You want your mommy? You are a disgrace! You disgust me!"

Carl did everything he could to refrain from what he wanted to do. Unfortunately, he couldn't. The senior cadet sealed his fate when he screamed out at the top of his lungs: "You are a disappointment to your dad!"

With that, Carl did something he had not done in so long. He clutched his fist and punched the senior cadet; it sent him to the ground. Carl was immediately apprehended and suspended. The Naval Academy sent Carl home with his walking papers: never to return.

Chapter 33
"Goodbye Boston"

Annie's Story:

Annie was surprised to get a midweek phone call from Carl. She was shocked to hear that he was back in Ohio. She was beyond disappointed to hear that Carl punched a senior officer. Annie knew there would always be a propensity of physical violence from Carl because of his upbringing. But never once was that violent side of Carl directed towards her. Carl kept it under control, but it was there. It was a part of his Ericsson heritage.

While finishing her sophomore year at Boston College, Annie filled out the necessary transfer papers and would head home to finish her degree and run for The University of Akron.

Carl drove to Boston to bring Annie home. It was a tearful reunion. After spending a few days in the city, they drove through New Jersey to visit Carl's relatives. Annie had gotten to know them quite well. Though Carl was often absent, Annie took the train to New Jersey frequently.

Arriving back in Ohio, Annie's parents had retired and moved south. Annie hoped that she and Carl would get a place together, but Arthur was in bad shape. Carl's mother asked if he would stay at home to help care for his dad.

Annie rented a small apartment close to the university and took a job-teaching summer school for the Akron Public Schools. She knew that Carl's place was with his mother right then. Still, she hoped that he would mention moving up their wedding date since they were both back home. Annie was also aware Carl would not want to leave his mother to carry the burden of tending to his dying father alone. And Carl especially would not want Annie living under the same roof with his father.

Annie was on cloud nine. She and Carl were inseparable. Being with Carl never got old and she could not wait to marry him. Annie wanted Carl in a physical way. The only thing stopping them was to be officially married. Mrs. Ericsson, or Mom as she insisted on being called, had designed and was sewing Annie's wedding dress. Annie was overjoyed that God's Will be in her favor. *"Things could not be more perfect."* Annie sighed.

Chapter 34
"A Dream Comes True"

Carl's and Annie's Story:

Though Carl shared with Annie the reason he was let go from the Naval Academy, he dared not say anything to his parents. Annie's disappointment was enough. One thing Carl learned from his parents was how to bury secrets. His mother had her plate full working full-time and trying to take care of Arthur.

When the question was asked about Carl leaving the academy, he would just say: "Apparently, some cadets were just dropping." Of course, he was referring to the senior cadet, he knocked out. Thankfully, most people believed it to mean the Navy was making cutbacks.

Besides, the Ericsson's had other things to worry about. Arthur's health was quickly diminishing. Time was not on his side. If anything, Arthur demonstrated what it meant to be a man. Never once did he complain about his condition. He tackled it with courage and character. The cancer seemed to have mellowed him. But then again, he was put through the ringer so to speak.

The surgeries along with his treatments eventually took their toll on him. He went from being a man of great strength and stature to nothing more than a skeleton.

Regardless, he was an Ericsson. And one thing Ericsson's did best was fight. He would fight this disease to the bitter end.

They say behind every storm cloud is a silver lining. With Carl and Annie now back together; Carl thought it best they move their wedding plans forward. One night, as Carl was able to escape from the confines of his father's care, he drove Annie to a spot of great significance.

Yes, you guessed it. It was the bridge where he face-planted his Annie. Beneath were the tracks where Annie would hear the train's whistle going to nowhere. On this particular evening, the tracks were in Annie's favor. Carl was going to make his and Annie's dreams come true.

He parked his car alongside the bridge. Annie had a puzzled look on her face.. "Carl, what on earth are you doing?" If there was one thing Carl learned about Annie was that she did not like surprises.

"Annie!" Carl pleaded. "I need you to get out of the car. There is something I need to ask you."

Annie being Annie had to insist. "Can't you just ask me in the car, Carl?"

"No! I can't" Carl retorted. "Please, Annie, do me the kind favor of doing as I ask."

Annie sensed Carl's urgency. She quietly removed herself from the passenger's seat, in protest, mind you.

"Follow me!" Carl instructed.

"Carl!" Annie's impatience was beginning to flare. But like a piece of metal is drawn to a magnet, Annie was drawn to Carl. She followed.

They stopped at precisely the same place where Carl kissed her so many years ago. He knelt down and re-proposed to Annie. With tears of joy, Carl re-asked the question. And as before, Annie accepted. There they fast-forwarded their origin plans. They moved their wedding date to a much earlier time. They both agreed to have the wedding at the community church next to their old elementary school.

In the book of fairy tales: dreams do come true. Carl embraced Annie only to say: "You are killing me so softly."

Chapter 35
"Killing Me Softly"

Annie's Story:

The rehearsal dinner was perfect. It was romantic and intimate. On a candle-lit deck overlooking the Portage Lakes, gathered Carl's family from Jersey, his parents, and Annie's soon-to-be brother-in-laws. Annie's parents were in town, but her brothers could not attend on short notice. Jill was Annie's Maid of Honor, and Allen would be standing with Carl. Like the dinner, the wedding in the morning would be a small and private affair. Annie did not like pomp and circumstance.

Like her father, Annie lived in sweats and running garb; but not tonight. For the first time in a long time, Annie felt beautiful and feminine. Marie helped Annie find the perfect dress for the evening. It was a dress that was modest but flattered Annie's figure. Marie picked up on Annie's flare for the 60's bohemian hippie look, and Annie's dress nailed it.

After dinner, Jill headed over to Annie's apartment. She was spending the night to help Annie get ready in the morning. Annie kissed her parents goodnight as they headed back to their hotel.

"Carl," Mrs. Ericsson said. "I'm making sure your aunts and your grandmother get settled in at The Quaker for the night. We'll be home soon."

She then turned to Annie and said "Your wedding dress is on a hook on the back of my bedroom door. Have Carl run you by the house to grab your dress." Marie gave Annie a hug. "See you in the morning my sweet daughter." Annie, Carl, and Allen headed home.

Carl's Story:

Yes, everything was perfect that evening. The last time Carl saw Annie stand out and shine was at Prom. Carl was not the only person to notice Annie's beauty, even Mr. Ericsson raised an eyebrow once or twice throughout the evening.. Since her return from Boston, Annie had become closer with Mr. Ericsson. However, drinking and drugs do not always make the perfect cocktail and Mr. Ericsson had indulged that night.

With Marie out, Annie had no reason to fear Mr. Ericsson. She bolted into the Ericsson home, taking the steps two at a time to grab her dress. Annie took the dress out of the plastic, admiring the beautiful work that Marie had put into it. What she was not prepared for was for Mr. Ericsson to burst into the bedroom and corner her.

Intoxicated, Mr. Ericsson took one look at Annie. She was beautiful. She was beyond beautiful. Arthur had a hard time to resist and restrain his innermost thoughts. "If my son isn't going to show you what it's like to be with a man, I will!"

Annie could tell the alcohol along with the medication had taken their effect on Mr. Ericsson. She tried to skirt his innuendos by stating: "Now dad! You don't mean that! You need to go to bed."

Arthur was not one for someone telling him what to do. Annie saw something in his eyes that night that she had not seen before. It was what his boys called the "Ericsson determination."

Determined to have his way, he grabbed Annie. A person would think a man dying of cancer had diminished strength. Think again. Mr. Ericsson, though he resembled a skeleton, was remarkably strong. Annie could not break free from his grip.

Annie knew all too well, what Mr. Ericsson was capable of. With Carl standing in the driveway, she cried out to him.

Like a bolt of lightning, he struck through the front door of the house. When he burst through the bedroom door, he found his Annie struggling with his father. Something clicked in Carl. Seeing Annie helpless, Carl remembered everything from that night of long, long ago.

The secrets buried deep within the ocean floor were stirred. They resurfaced. Carl now recalled his father busting through the bathroom door. He now remembered how his father cocked his arm back only to belt him across the head with his "slap stick."

He saw the fear in Annie's eyes. "Not this time, father! Let her go!" Carl snapped.

Arthur shot back in his delirious state: "You think you are man enough, boy?"

"Old man, I know I am man enough!" Carl said without intimidation. "Let Annie go!" He ordered.

Unbelievably, Arthur abided. He let Annie go. "Well, let's see what you got, boy!"

Carl grinned. "With pleasure!" He belted his dying father across the left cheek. Annie stood in shock.

She could not believe what was to happen next. Arthur snapped his head back to face his son. "Boy, that's the last time you will ever strike your father." From on top of the dresser, the old man picked up his shotgun and struck Carl between the eyes with the butt end.

As if in slow motion, Annie watched in horror as Carl's body went limp and slumped to the floor. The gun discharged and sent Arthur flying backwards. Arthur hit his head and now lay on the floor next to Carl. Hearing a gun discharge from the Ericsson house was typically not a big deal, but Allen decided he'd better check it out.

Allen fell to his knees at the scene before him. Annie howled hysterically while cradling Carl's lifeless body. Arthur was sprawled across the floor next to him. Now home and hearing the commotion, Marie joined Allen on her knees and wept over Carl and Annie.

Allen left the room, leaving the two women time to grieve. Upon returning, he picked Annie up off the floor and placed her in the arms of his mother. Allen gave Annie a moment with Marie. Marie whispered into Annie's ear and then Allen whisked Annie away from the house. Allen would do, what he did best. Allen was left to clean up the mess created by his father. And once again, Allen would have to take care of his younger twin. There would be more secrets for the Ericsson clan to bury this night.

Later that night, Allen found Annie standing on the railroad bridge deep in thought. They reminisced about the fight she and Carl had on the bridge; the face plant kiss and Carl's painful punch. Annie fished something out of her pocket and showed it to Allen. He nodded his head in affirmation and drove Annie home

Chapter 36
"Left at the Altar"

Annie's Story:

The morning of the wedding was Annie's first official act in accordance with the Ericcson Code of Conduct.

Jill fussed over Annie as she helped her dress for the wedding. The guests had arrived at the tiny little church. A pianist played the songs that had special meaning to Carl and Annie.

Carl's mother and father were escorted down the aisle and seated. After giving Annie a kiss, her mother was seated next to Marie and Arthur. Allen paced. The minister looked at his watch. The guests started to whisper amongst themselves.

Annie stood in front of the stained glass window while the sunlight danced in colorful rays across the carpet. Masking her grief and her anger, Annie held her head high. Standing arm-in-arm with her father, Annie was stoic. For in her heart, she was already married to Carl. She married Carl in the presence of these dancing sunrays some ten years ago.

Annie made her apologies and thanked her guests for coming. As Marie and Arthur left the church, Annie almost felt sorry for the old man. Arthur had no recollection of the evening before. He was in complete disbelief that his son had left Annie standing at the altar.

Annie was an Ericsson. "Famiglia" as Marie had whispered in Annie's ear the night Carl died. Annie would not bring shame or scandal to the Ericsson name. Annie was family. She became clan the moment she let Carl into her heart. And the Ericsson clan had secrets. Annie's last testament of her love for Carl was not sending his father to prison where he would have died alone of guilt and shame.

On the way home from the church, Arthur could not help but to dwell upon the absence of his son at his own wedding. He knew that Carl's love for Annie ran deep.

Arthur's mind was often clouded by medication and alcohol. He had a vague image of an altercation with Carl the night before. But his mind would not let him remember.

"What have I done Marie?" Arthur cried out. "Did I drive our boy away from Annie? Am I so bad that I drove him away?"

Unable to contain herself, Marie pulled the car over. "Arthur, Arthur, you killed our boy. Carl is dead because…"

Arthur finished her sentence "Because I killed him." A sense of urgency overcame Arthur. "Take me back to the church." He pleaded with Marie.

Marie turned the car around and walked Arthur back into the church. He fell on his knees in front of the great stained glass window; the window where Carl professed his love to Annie. It was the window that brought closure for Annie and it would be the same window that would bring redemption to Arthur. On his knees in front of the patchwork glass Jesus, Arthur cried. He cried out for his Heavenly Father to bring release to the sin in his heart.

"Forgive me. Forgive me." Arthur thought about all the people that had been hurt by his actions. The wrongs he committed against his sons, his wife, and Carl's beautiful Annie. How would Annie ever forgive him?

"Arthur, let me help you up," Marie said, trying to comfort her husband.

"I need to make things right between me and my God." Arthur spoke to Jesus and felt the blessing of absolution upon him. He walked out of the church believing he was right with the Lord.

Arthur felt joy in his heart, but he also felt sickened by what he did to Annie. Though Annie was willing to set Arthur free, Arthur told Marie that he was going to turn himself in.

Arthur confessed his crime to the authorities. He shortly died in his sleep. He made things right with Jesus. He made things right with the authorities. Unfortunately, he never got the opportunity to make things right with Annie.

Chapter 37
"The Golden Years"

Out on her porch, Annie plopped down in her rocking chair. She leaned her head back and closed her eyes. A gentle breeze rustled the trees on the humid summer evening. Annie listened to the cows mooing in a nearby pasture. She heard the rumble and then the whistle of the 7:00 freight train roll by. Annie was enjoying the moment; reflecting on her past forty years of teaching for the Trenton, NJ School District and now settling into retirement.

The sound of a car making its way down the long gravel driveway made Annie get up from her chair. "Oh Carly." She said, "What a lovely surprise. What brings you out this way?"

Carly was Annie's niece and Goddaughter. She was the grown daughter of Jill and Allen.

"Husband issues. I had to get out of the house and my path brought me here." She replied.

"Love can be painful Carly." Annie said, wrapping her arm around her niece. "Walk with me," Annie continued as they crossed through the meadow behind Annie's house. "Do you have time to listen to your old aunt's story about true love; unadulterated love?" She asked Carly

Annie and Carly took a seat on a swing in the back of the yard. Next to the swing was Annie's beautifully tended flower garden. "My story of love started with a swing, and ended in that garden." Annie said, pointing to her flowers. With misty eyes, Carly sat and listened as Annie told her an incredible story about love – and her Uncle Carl, her dad's twin for whom she was named in honor of.

Several hours later, Carly left and Annie went back inside the house. She had many blessings in life. Carly was one of them; a niece near and dear to her heart.

Before going to bed, Annie flipped open her Bible, a gift from Marie. Gingerly she removed a torn yellowed paper napkin; a napkin Annie had picked up many years ago. She unfolded it and traced her fingers along what was left of the faded red letters; C-A-R-L. At the bottom of the napkin in smaller print was, *"Hoboken, NJ"*. A tattered napkin from a Carl's Jr. restaurant carelessly tossed out a car window the night before her wedding day, lead Annie and Carl to New Jersey. Here on a farm in New Jersey, Carl remained next to Annie's swing until her own death years later.

Made in the USA
Lexington, KY
07 October 2015